PRAISE FOR *ISABEL OF THE WHALES:*

"Fantasy and reality merge in this aquatic coming-of-age adventure with a compelling ecological message…To Velmans's credit, the improbable seems probable through the eyes and voice of her down-to-earth heroine.
"Watch out, *Little Mermaid,* here comes ISABEL!"
— *Kirkus Reviews*

"The fantasy elements are eclipsed by the real magic of whale life. Isabel's pack is presented in detail, each character realized and believable, and the book's pacing and mood highlight the dangers of storms and comforts of humpbacks' communal existence."
— *School Library Journal*

"Remarkably insightful look into life as a whale. While the book is directed at younger readers at a 9-12-year-old level, I learned a lot about whales and I'm 16!"
— *Young Adults Book Central*

"Elements of the tale are endearing, and taken as a whole, *Isabel of the Whales* is a lovely, evocative story."
— Carolynn Evans, *Curled Up With a Good Kid's Book*

Killingly Memorial School's **One School, One Book** *Selection*

D0180335

Jessaloup's Song

HESTER VELMANS

van Horton Books

Jessaloup's Song is a work of fiction. Any resemblance to any person or whale is purely coincidental.

Published by van Horton Books

ISBN 978-0-9835505-9-4

Jacket illustration by Jesse Reisch

For Peter

Once I sat upon a promontory
and heard a mermaid on a dolphin's back
uttering such dulcet and harmonious breath
that the rude sea grew civil at her song
and certain stars shot madly from their spheres
to hear the sea-maid's music

— William Shakespeare,
A Midsummer Night's Dream

Here they come: one by one, in two long snaking lines. The young whales first, jostling one another to be in front. Behind them the families, the mothers with their half-yearlings. Finally the elders come sweeping up alongside: Momboduno, with Onijonah on his right; Bonadiboh, Lord of the Ice Floe, and General Trogulo, the old battle-scarred warrior, on his left. As they pass him, each gazes deep into his unblinking eye.

Although he is anxious to be off, to start on his fearful adventure, he patiently endures the endless farewell. For each member of the tribe must be given a chance to donate a token of fortitude to the great store of courage he will be needing to complete his quest. It is ordained in the Song.

Even the seaweed is waving farewell. The light above has faded to a dusky, ominous green. He blinks, makes an effort to stay still in the prescribed position, although he is itching to flap his flukes, to shake his head, to twist his body and release some of the pent-up energy that has been building up in him and is about ready to explode.

There, at last, is Indigoneah, Keeper of Songs. As always, she is the last in line. Instead of gliding past him, she stops as she draws up alongside. He can sense the whales behind him settling into their positions. Without needing to look, he can tell that they are drawn up in great concentric semi-circles back there, like tiers of spectators in a Roman theater.

Nobody moves. There is a thick, expectant hush. The whole ocean seems to be holding its breath.

Then, finally:

"Courage, my son," Indigoneah intones.

"Courage," comes a hushed whisper from the whales behind him.

"Follow the Way of the Song," she continues.

"Follow the Way of the Song," hums the chorus at his back.

"May you succeed in your task," rumbles Indigoneah.

"Succeed in your task," sings the chorus, louder now.

"May you survive unharmed!" she bellows.

"SurVIVE unHARMED!" It's a deafening roar.

An involuntary shiver twitches all up and down his spine.

"Go now," Indigoneah exhorts him, "and make us proud. Save the HUMANS!"

The cry "SAVE THE HUMANS!" lifts him up on a tidal wave of sound as he sets off in the opposite direction, and it goes on ringing in his ears for many a mile as he makes his long, lonely way toward the shore.

one

OFTEN at night, with the wind rattling my window and the rustling branches outside swelling, crashing and ebbing away again like the sea, I'd suddenly find myself sitting up in bed, wide awake. Joy and sadness inflated my stomach like a balloon, and next thing I knew, I was kneeling at the window — my turret window, at the top of my family's blue Victorian house on Cape Cod. Once my eyes had grown used to the dark, I was able to make out the sliver of sea that was *my* sea, the narrow slice of ocean wedged between the hardware store and the marina. I could kneel there for hours, until my knees were numb and my eyes dry from staring.

What I was hoping to see out there was clearly impossible — it was too far away, and too dark, and too deep. Still I would keep waiting, and yearning... hoping. There! That glint on the horizon, gone in a flash. Could it be...?

And then, warmed in the pit of my stomach by that little crumb of hope, I would finally crawl back into my bed, and shut my eyes. And I dreamed I was being called back to the sea.

two

"ISABEL! Are you dreaming, Isabel? I asked you a question!"

I looked up, startled. Mrs. Stiglitz was mouthing words at me, words that echoed hollowly in the neon-lit classroom. There were charts on the wall, a whiteboard, kids slumped all around me in little desks. There was a notebook open in front of me, I seemed to have a pencil in my hand, a pencil with a tassel on the end of it, but for a moment I had no idea what I was supposed to be doing.

"Uh... Could you repeat the question, please?" I stammered.

"I said, have you got your final assignment for me? Everyone else has handed it in except you."

I fumbled around, peered under the book on my desk. Sure enough, there was a sheaf of papers, paper-clipped together, hiding underneath. I pulled it out and, pushing myself sideways out of my desk, stumbled to the front of the classroom.

"Sorry," I muttered, handing her my assignment. The bell had rung, and everyone was making for the door.

"Isabel. A word." Mrs. Stiglitz's voice was stern.

"I have to get to Spanish class…" I said feebly.

"I don't know what is *with* you these days. You were always such an excellent student. Now you're constantly off in some never-never land, it seems. And your work is suffering. You're just not concentrating enough. Are you getting enough sleep? I shall have to speak to your parents."

I mumbled something about insomnia, and escaped.

In the corridor, I ran into Tom, my ex-boyfriend. I'd broken up with him weeks ago, but he still acted as if he hadn't gotten the memo. "Hey, Isabel," he said. "What's up!"

"I'm late for class," I panted.

"Haven't seen you around at all," he said reproachfully. "You avoiding me, or what? Battle of the Bands day after tomorrow, you know."

"I know!" I yelled over my shoulder.

"Don't forget!" he shouted after me. "You gotta be there! Promise!"

In Spanish class, my best friend Molly had saved me a seat. She looked at me quizzically.

"The Stick has it in for me again. She says she's going to have to talk to my parents," I moaned. "I'm 'just not concentrating enough', she says."

"Well it's true," Molly said, "you do seem kind of out of it."

"And Tom keeps bugging me about the Battle of the Bands."

"Come on, aren't you even a little excited about Tom and his band? They've got a good chance of winning, you know."

I shrugged. "He acts as if we're still together. I mean, as if he didn't even *hear* me when I told him I wanted to break up."

"I don't think he believes that's the way you really feel. He thinks you'll change your mind, especially if his band wins."

"So what am I supposed to do? Pretend everything's fine, and scream my head off when it's his turn to play?"

"Plenty of girls would love to take your place, you know," said Molly. "Everyone thinks he's *way* cool."

"I know," I sighed. "It's just me, I guess."

Molly patted my hand. "You can't help feeling the way you feel. But I do wish you wouldn't act so gloomy. Cheer up, can't you? I mean, we're nearly done for the year. Almost three whole months of freedom ahead of us! What is *up* with you anyway?"

"Nothing's up," I shrugged, rifling through the stack of

books before me to find my Spanish textbook. "*Nada,* uh, *esta arriba,*" I clarified in my best stab at Spanish, pointing up at the ceiling and snapping my fingers. "*Olé!*"

Molly snorted. "You make me laugh, *Señorita.*"

"I do?" I said.

"You still do," she said. "Sometimes."

three

BUT it was true, I was feeling gloomy. I had nothing to cheer up about.

Today was the anniversary. Three years!

That was what was so upsetting: it had been three whole years, and I was still leading this perfectly predictable, perfectly uneventful landlubber life.

Three years of carrying a secret I couldn't share with anyone.

Three years since something had turned my world upside down.

Three years since I was changed forever.

Something had happened to me three years ago, something that had changed everything, and people kept expecting me to get over it, to forget it, to put it behind me. My friends. My parents. My brothers. I felt bad about letting them down, but I couldn't help it. I felt different.

I had tried for a while to get along with Tom, flattered that he liked me. I'd tried to be this happy, cheerful, *grateful* girlfriend he expected me to be, but it kept getting harder and harder. In the end I just gave up, because I realized Tom and I weren't at all interested in the same things. We didn't even like the same music. He always made me feel whatever *he* was doing was more important than what *I* wanted to do.

And what I wanted to do was sit on the jetty somewhere. All I wanted to do was dive into the waves and go for a long swim, or sit on the beach and stare out at the sea.

My parents didn't like me going swimming. Actually, they didn't want me going anywhere near the sea these days. If it was hot, I was allowed to go swim in a friend's pool, but I had to get special permission to go to the beach, and I was absolutely forbidden to go on a boat, any boat, *ever* — whether it was a sailboat, a ferry, or even a dinghy, anything that bobbed up and down in the water was a no-no. *So* unfair! So I was constantly sneaking around behind my parents' backs. It bothered me that I had to lie to them, but the ocean kept pulling me back.

That wasn't the only thing we were butting heads about. When I came home I'd head straight up to my room on the third floor, my sea-green cocoon, where I felt snug and safe. My parents didn't understand why I didn't hang out downstairs with them. I wished they would just come out and say it, I wished they would yell at me for being such a pill, I wished they didn't think that I'd get over it. They were so sure that this was just a phase, that it would pass, that I'd grow up a bit and in the end I'd be happy living in *their* world again.

I wished I thought they were right. But I didn't.

You know what it's like to go through a turnstile — you're on one side of the barrier, you push the slick, cold metal bar in front of you and — *click* — you're suddenly through to the other side? Well, that's what it was like, for me. Before, and After.

On one side of my life, the past side of my life, I had been an ordinary, happy-go-lucky girl living an ordinary, happy-go-lucky life in Provincetown, trying to please my teachers (sometimes), squabbling with my brothers and having fun with my friends, hanging out in my turret-room, teaching myself the guitar, sitting down for meals with my family, shopping for clothes, listening to music, texting and I-M-ing and all that stuff. I was content, I suppose: I just took it all for granted. I didn't know any better.

And then this thing happened — *click* — I passed through that turnstile, and found myself in a whole other world, living a very, very different life, and experiencing a very, very different kind of happiness. (Thinking about that happiness now really hurt. It felt like two fists pressing on my chest so that I could hardly breathe. How come the memory of being so happy can make you feel so bad?)

Then, a year later, I was forced to go back again — *click*, back through the turnstile — and, even though it was all as it had been before, everything had changed. Suddenly my life, my regular, ordinary life, struck me as weird, or maybe just different — just one possibility out of thousands of other possibilities, thousands of other ways to live on this planet.

Sometimes, in the middle of brushing my teeth, I'd freeze, and stare at the toothbrush. What was that thing in my hand? Why was I jiggling it that way inside my mouth, spitting out foam? Who was that creature in the mirror, the one with strands of straight brown hair on either side of her cheeks, with a nose and two nostril holes, and two furry arches above her eyes — what were eyebrows *for*, anyway?

You can make yourself crazy that way.

four

It had started innocently enough. At our school, the fifth grade traditionally went on a whale watch, an outing I had been looking forward to ever since I could remember. I knew more about whales than anyone else in my class. Even as a little girl I had always been obsessed with whales. I read about them, I had a stuffed-animal collection of them, I wrote reports about them for school. And I often dreamed about them.

I remember how excited I was the morning of the whale watch, three years ago. I had this strange feeling bubbling up in the pit of my stomach that something important was going to happen.

Once we were out at sea, Mr. Peake, our teacher, told us we'd have to be patient, and for a long time we didn't see anything except gulls. But then, suddenly, the most amazing thing happened.

The sea seemed to come alive!

From one moment to the next, we were surrounded by a great ring of spouting, whooshing, grey and black bodies — hundreds of them. As far as the eye could see. Even the boat's crew had never seen so many whales all in one place. The whales were pressing in on the boat, as if they wouldn't let us pass. All the other kids and adults on board were scared, but I remember just feeling excited. I felt an immediate affinity with those great animals; I thought they were trying to tell us something.

Then, while trying to take their picture, I leaned out too far… just as the boat was rammed from behind. My camera slipped out of my hand, I made a grab for it — and I fell overboard.

I thought it was an accident, but later I wasn't so sure.

I'm told that the Coast Guard put on a huge search for me after I went down, but they found no trace of me anywhere. I had vanished without a trace. In the end they'd had to give up and call off the search. Everybody assumed that I had drowned.

But I didn't drown.

Right after hitting the water, I was transformed. I blew up into this huge whale. I don't know how it happened. It just did. It sounds crazy, I know, but it's true. In a matter of seconds, I turned from an eighty-pound girl into a *forty-*

thousand-pound humpback whale!

Compared to the other whales, I wasn't even that big. I wasn't full grown, of course. Some of them were twice as big as me.

But the most amazing thing was that the whales had been expecting me. They had known I was coming. They said I was a Chosen One — that's a human who is destined to come to them. It was foretold in their Song, they said.

Once I got over my bewilderment — how could something like this ever *happen*? — I decided to make the best of it. I had no other choice.

I lived with my whale family — my pod — for one whole summer and one whole winter. I tagged along when they migrated up north to feed and stock up on blubber, and then I swam with them all the way south, to the place the whales call Home, where they mate and breed. They taught me their language, their ways, and their history. I learned to be resourceful in ways I had never dreamed of, and even though I did sometimes miss my family and friends back on land, I grew closer and closer to the whales who were now my family. I loved my life out there in the vastness of the ocean. I can't even begin to describe what it meant to me, being accepted by the whales, and learning all about their awesome way of life. I even found out the significance of their Song.

But then I had a close call. On our return journey north we were attacked, first by a whaling ship and then by sharks. I managed to stop the whaling ship by jamming a wooden boom into the rudder, but my tail was badly injured in the process. The wound became infected, and the elders decided that the only way to save my life was to send me back to dry land, where I could be treated by human doctors, in a hospital. I didn't want to go, but they insisted; they said I would die if I stayed.

So in the end I had no choice. I beached myself and – lo and behold — I turned back into a girl. The whole thing sounds incredible, I know, but it really happened.

At first, once my leg was healed, I was kind of happy to be home. I had missed my family, and they were so overjoyed to have me back. But it wasn't long before I started being desperately homesick for my *other* family — Onijonah, my whale guardian, and Mistenbel, her baby, and most of all Jessaloup, the coolest young whale you'll ever meet. So much cooler than any of the boys at our school.

And the worst thing was that I had to lie to everyone about what happened to me after I fell overboard. I told them that I'd been washed up on some desert island, and survived like Robinson Crusoe. I told them that in the end I had made myself a raft that brought me home. I thought people would think I was completely cuckoo if I told them that I had turned into a whale. I mean, who wants to end up in an insane asylum?

So here I was, with my big secret, pretending to be "normal". Whatever that meant.

five

WHEN I got home from school, my mother looked up from her computer at the desk in the kitchen and asked me, as always, how my day had gone. I shrugged. "OK, I guess."

"Are you sure? I had a call from one of your teachers — Mrs. Stiglitz? She wants to have a conference with Dad and me before school is out —"

I let out a groan. "I'm still getting A's and B's, I don't see why…"

"But Isabel, she's not the only one who is concerned about you. You seem to be in this dream world lately, walking around like a zombie. And school's almost out, and you haven't made any plans for the summer yet, have you."

"Whatever," I said.

"You know your dad and I expect you to find a job. You can't just hang around here all summer."

"I know," I said.

"Is something up? Can't you tell me what's wrong? Are things still OK between you and Tom?"

I sighed. My mother was always probing, always trying to get me to talk. I remember when I used to tell her everything. But it was getting harder and harder. I hadn't even told her about breaking up with Tom. I didn't think she would understand what I was going through, and I didn't want to have to deal with her questions.

My brother Jacob came storming in just at that moment, cutting the interrogation short. He was waving his cell phone in the air. "Joey just called me. Everyone's up at Race Point Beach. There's a stranded whale…"

Suddenly there was such a banging in my chest that I thought I was going to *pass out*.

"A… *WHAT?*" I cried.

"A whale. Beached itself. Gotta check it out, dude."

"Wait! It could be dangerous —" my mother began. Jacob, heading for the door, told her not to worry. "It's fine, Mom. There's a whole crowd there already. I'll be careful." His booming voice sounded so confident, so like Dad's, that she caved in immediately with a weak, "Well, if you're sure…" If it had been *me* asking, she would have put up a huge fuss. She hated to let me out of her sight these days.

"Mom!" I cried. "I'm going too!"

"Isabel, I'd rather you stayed here. You know we don't like you going near the... I'd rather you didn't go to the beach."

"That's *so* not fair! *Why* won't you let me go? If *he's* allowed to go, then *I* should be allowed to go too! What is *wrong* with me going to the beach?"

My mother hesitated, as if she was about to explain something. But she didn't. She looked at me guiltily. Then she said, "Well, all right then, I guess. Go. But don't go in the ocean, and don't go anywhere near the whale, you could get crushed. And I want you both back in time for dinner. Understand? Jacob — keep an eye on your sister!" she shouted, pushing open the screen door.

"Wait, Jacob!" I yelled. I grabbed my backpack that happened to have my bathing suit in it, squeezed past her in the doorway and ran down the steps. "Wait for me, I'm coming too!"

"Sure you are," he said. "Is that how you ask?"

Jacob was a senior, and he had a car. At fourteen going on fifteen, I wasn't old enough yet to drive. That was why I had to suck up to him whenever I needed a ride. But I wasn't in a mood to go, you know, all *p-pretty-please...?* I jumped in the passenger seat of his Jeep.

"You'll have to get in the back. We've got to pick up Stephanie first."

I wasn't in the mood to argue either, especially when it came to his *darling* girlfriend Stephanie. I dived into the back, my mind racing. Which whale? Was it one I knew?

What if he or she was dead, or dying? I had this bad, really bad feeling churning in my stomach.

"Did Joey say what kind of whale it was?" I asked.

"He didn't know, but he did say it's much bigger than the pilot whales that beached themselves a couple of years ago. It's probably a humpback, from his description."

At Stephanie's house we had to wait at least five minutes for Jacob's girlfriend to make an appearance. I was going out of my mind. I thought I might have to puke. "Come on, hurry up, Stephanie!" I yelled.

"Stop banging the back of my seat," Jacob said.

"I'm just changing into my suit," I told him. "Don't look."

"You're not supposed to go in the ocean," he reminded me.

"I know. But that's so unfair, you've said so yourself!" I complained, wriggling into my bathing suit and then putting my sweat pants and hoodie back on. It wasn't exactly a sweltering day.

"Yeah, I know they're being a bit unreasonable about it. You're a good swimmer, I'll give you that, but hey…"

I looked around. My neck felt stiff and tense. Still no sign of Stephanie. "Can't we *go* now?"

"We'll get there when we get there," he said.

"Oh yeah? What if we're too late?" I snapped.

"If the whale really got itself stuck high and dry, it's going to be there for a good long time," he said condescendingly, suddenly the big expert on marine life. "It's almost impossible to get them to turn round and swim back out to sea. They're too dumb to find their way back."

I was fuming, but kept my mouth shut. I remembered all too well what it felt like, being beached. It had happened to me. Like drowning in the dry sand, suffocating under your own weight. Like being forced to lie on a bed of a gazillion sharp nails.

Stephanie finally came sashaying out of her house. She was wearing a spaghetti-strap top and shorts, and gobs of makeup.

"OK, let's go!" I said.

Stephanie ignored me. "We have to pick up Jenny first," she told my brother. "She wants to come too. And let's stop for a sandwich, I'm hungry."

"Oh, great!" I yelled. "Let me off here, in that case. I'll just get there myself!"

"Fine. Whatever."

Jacob stopped at the corner of our street and I jumped out. I raced back to my house, darted into the shed and pulled out my bike. Pedaling down the street as hard as I could, I headed for Race Point beach, moaning, "*Please — please — please — don't let me get there too late...*"

six

Almost fifteen minutes later, my lungs bursting and my legs burning, I pulled up to the beach parking lot. I flung my bike on the ground, kicked off my shoes and sprinted barefoot along the path through the dunes. I saw people standing in a group down by the water line, scratching their heads, pointing. They were peering at a large dark object partially sticking up out of the water.

A very large object.

A large, immobile, torpedo-shaped object with scalloped, white-tipped flippers that, rocked by the waves, bobbed around a little on the surface...

I'd have recognized those flippers anywhere. My legs buckled under me. I landed on the sand with a hard plop.

For a moment I didn't know where I was.

I blinked. I was sitting on the sand, my legs sprawled out in front of me. Down the beach, the crowd of gaping bystanders hadn't noticed me. I didn't know if it was from the wind or the shock, but I felt tears drying on either side of my cheeks, tickling my earlobes. I scrambled to my feet. The old scar on my right leg pulling and throbbing, I started loping awkwardly down the beach, down to the water.

As I drew closer, I knew there was no mistake. It was Jessaloup, my best buddy. The awesomest, most athletic whale in our pod of humpbacks, or, as they prefer to call themselves, Sirens: The Singing Ones. Jessaloup, the whale I had never stopped thinking about, not a single day since I'd found myself back on dry land, three terribly long years ago. It was Jessaloup, and he was hurt, he was in trouble, he was dying…

"Hey, watch out there Miss — Where you goin'? Don't you go no closer!" A man in a baseball cap held out his arms to stop me from wading into the water. "It's dangerous!"

My anxiety turned to rage — fury at this man who knew nothing, nothing, *nothing* at all. I was so angry that I couldn't get any words out. I just elbowed him out of my way and splashed past him as if I hadn't heard him.

There he was – Jessaloup, lying flat in the surf. Waves crashed over his back, and with every surge, his flippers rocked up and down like two great inflatable pool toys. At least he was alive — a weak puff of spray came bubbling out of his blowholes every thirty seconds or so. The rest of him wasn't moving at all — his jaw, his pleated belly, were stuck in the sand; I saw that he was pinned to the bottom by the undertow. I waded over to his right side, reached out my hand, and touched him. His great eye, just below the water line, was closed.

"Jessaloup," I whispered.

The eye opened, and gazed at me.

"It's me, Isabel. I'm here."

The eye blinked. Then again.

"It's *me*, Jessaloup. Say something!"

I heard a faint click-rumble, somewhere deep inside.

He knew.

"Oh, Jessaloup, what are you *doing* here!" I groaned. "What were you *thinking?*"

seven

THERE must be a reason, I thought to myself wildly. Jessaloup would never accidentally beach himself. Jessaloup would never get himself into a fix like this... Was it because of me?

Had he missed me as much as I'd missed him?

I touched him — gently, I didn't want to put any more pressure on him. I stretched my arm up to stroke his head. The part I could reach felt dry. Too dry. I cupped my hands and started splashing seawater over him, taking care to avoid his blowholes.

I sensed a commotion behind me. I turned to look at the beach. The crowd was gesturing at me wildly. Then I saw that one of the desperately waving people was Jacob, and he was splashing through the surf toward me. In less than ten seconds he was at my elbow. Before I could explain, he tackled me, and, grabbing my arm in a viselike grip, hauled me back onto the beach. I fought back, but he was too strong for me.

"Stop!" I yelled, trying to kick at his legs. "Stop it, Jacob! Let me go!"

"What are you *doing?*" Jacob hissed. "Didn't you hear what Mom said? It's dangerous to get so close! That thing could roll over on top of you, it could kill you with a flip of its tail!"

"No! Get off me, you jerk! Let me go!"

Next thing I knew I was on my back on the sand looking up at him, gasping for breath. He had my wrists pinned above my head and was holding down my legs with his knee. We'd been rolling around in the sand, fighting like little kids.

Jacob backed off, sat back on his haunches and then got to his feet. "Cut it out, stupid. You're making a complete ass of yourself!"

"Who, me? I was just..." I sobbed. "You don't understand..." I gave up, helpless. I didn't even know where to begin explaining to him what he didn't understand.

The crowd had turned its back on the sea in order to stare at the two of us. Scrubbing at my tears, I struggled to my feet, suddenly horribly self-conscious. Stephanie and Jenny had their hands over their mouths, stifling giggles. I smiled sheepishly at them, slapping the sand off my shorts.

Just then a huge wave crashed way up onto the beach where we were standing; I tottered, nearly losing my footing again. The tide was coming in.

There was a shout.

"Hey — Look! What the…? Where'd he go?" someone was yelling.

All heads swiveled back to the water. Out there, where a minute ago everyone had clearly seen the broad back of a massive whale, there was nothing but… sea. Waves. Horizon.

"Where did it go? It's gone!" people were yelling. "The whale's swum off!"

"Must have been that big wave just now," said the man who had tried to stop me from getting close. He lifted his baseball cap to scratch the bald spot on the top of his head. "That's what did it. Tide coming in. Must have given it just enough of a cushion to let it swim away."

"Where is it? Can you still *see* it anywhere?" squealed Stephanie, hanging on to Jacob's shoulder.

Everyone was staring at the water, hoping to see a tail, a spout, somewhere out there.

Finally Jacob shrugged. "It's gone. Too bad. Well, good for the whale, I say. Let's hope it's learned its lesson, not to come in so close again."

My heart was beating so wildly in my chest that I was sure everyone could tell. I was about to explode. Except that no one was looking my way. No one was looking in the direction *I* was looking in. No one saw what *I* saw.

Out there, just beyond the crashing surf, there was something in the waves. Or, rather, someone. A boy. Just some kid out for a swim; nothing out of the ordinary. None of the people on the beach paid any attention.

Except for me. Because there was something very familiar about that dark head bobbing in the waves.

The crowd started to disperse. "Come on, Steph, Jenny," said Jacob. "Let's go. Nothing to see here anymore. You coming, Izza?"

I shook my head.

"I'm sorry I was a little rough with you, just now," my brother said. "I was only trying to protect you…"

"I know. It's OK, don't worry. You guys go on ahead. I think I'll stay for a while. I feel like going for a swim," I said as nonchalantly as I could.

"What, are you crazy? It's not even July yet! The water's too cold!" Jenny squealed.

"She doesn't mind, do you, Izz?" Jacob said, kind of proudly. "My sister's like those polar-bear club nut jobs. She'll swim in any kind of weather. Although she's not supposed to."

"What do you mean, she's not supposed to?" asked Jenny.

"My parents have this thing about Isabel going near the water," Jacob explained. "They're kind of paranoid about it."

"But why?" said Jenny. "I mean, if she's such a good swimmer?"

Jacob shrugged. "Just some weird notion my parents

have."

"Isabel almost drowned once, when she went on a whale watch with her class," Stephanie informed Jenny. "Before you moved here, Jen."

"That explains it," said Jen.

"Yeah," said Jacob.

I had already wriggled out of my clothes, leaving them in a pile on the sand. "Don't tell on me, all right?" I begged.

"Do I ever? See you at home then. Don't be late, you'll get me in trouble. You know Mom will kill me if she finds out."

"I won't say anything if *you* don't," I said.

"Deal." My brother, Stephanie and Jenny started trudging back to the parking lot with the rest of the crowd.

I ran into the surf. The cold water snapped at my skin like a stack of rubber bands. In less than a minute I was within a few feet of the boy – the *human* boy — bobbing up and down in the waves.

"Jessaloup?" I whispered. "Is that *you?*"

eight

HE didn't answer. But I knew it was him. The eyes. I'd have known those large, wide-set eyes anywhere. They were looking a bit panicky.

"Come on," I said. "Let's get out of the water."

His eyes grew even wider.

I took hold of his arm, and pulled. "Come on. Being on land won't hurt, I promise. Just follow me."

I turned toward shore and caught a wave, keeping a grip on his arm. His *human* arm! When we hit the gravel strip I stumbled to my feet, but he stayed in the surf, on his stomach, the waves lapping over him.

"It's OK," I shouted at him. "You're not stuck. Try it. You can get out."

He started pushing himself up on his arms, and it suddenly occurred to me that he was naked.

"Oh — wait," I yelled. "Stay there. I'll get you some clothes." I ran back to where I had left my sweats, and returned to Jessaloup with them. "Here," I said, and then, when I saw that he still didn't understand, I showed him, by putting my right leg into one pant leg, and then the left. Then I pulled them off again. "Now you try," I told him.

He sat up, with his back to me, and tried to pull on the pants. After an awkward struggle he managed to get them on, although they were much too short on him.

I shook my head. I was suddenly feeling very short of breath, and I felt tears springing into my eyes. I couldn't believe it. Was this really happening? Jessaloup, here beside me? My head was spinning...

A big wave came skidding sideways up toward where we were sitting, splashed around our feet and ankles, then slid back into the thirsty sand.

"Come on," I said, hooking my arms under his armpits from behind, because I realized he didn't know how to walk. "This way." I started dragging him backwards up the beach, onto dry sand. I couldn't make it more than a few feet, though, because he was pretty heavy.

I sprawled in the sand next to him. "Say something!"

He opened his mouth. A low, growling noise came out.

I was going to have to teach him everything.

nine

WHEN I had first turned into a whale, I too had had to learn everything from scratch — how to swim, how to dive, how to navigate, how to feed, even how to sleep so as not to drown. Because even whales can drown, if they don't come up for air. They put me in a class with the yearlings. It was like being sent back to kindergarten. It was humiliating. So I knew just how he felt.

"Just nod your head — like this — if you understand me. OK?"

Jessaloup nodded his head. But, I suddenly thought, panicked, what if he's just copying me like a parrot, and he doesn't really know what I'm saying?

"Do you know that I'm Isabel?" I asked.

He nodded. And again, vehemently.

I turned my head away, because I didn't want him to see the tears that I felt prickling my eyes again.

I took a deep breath and started again. "Do you understand what's happened to you?"

Another nod. I felt his hand on my arm. I gazed down at it. His hand was warm. His skin was dark, almost as dark as his whale skin, but the palm of his hand was almost white, like his flippers and flukes. Resting my cheek on my knees, I peeked sideways at his face. It was different — a boy's face. A serious face. A handsome face, I couldn't help noticing — but what did I expect? Now that he was a boy, not a whale, he looked different, of course, yet everything about him was familiar to me. Even the matted black hair, which fell in wet dreadlocks in his face. Everything about him was just — Jessaloup. The way I remembered him. Especially his eyes, clear as sea glass…

He was waving his hand at me. His other hand, the left one. He was shaking it, wanting me to look.

I stared at it in shock. It was — *oh no!* Not a hand. Not a human hand, anyway. The long, knobby fingers, except for the thumb, were webbed and fused together at the tips. I touched it gingerly. It felt just like his other hand, only it *looked* like a flipper. The tip of Jessaloup's pectoral fin. Only a lot smaller.

He stared at it ruefully. "Oh dear," I said.

He started poking it with his other, normal hand.

"Yes, I see it. But it's no big deal, Jessaloup. It hardly shows."

He hung his head.

"It's OK, really," I comforted him. "We'll make it so no one will notice."

A seagull sailed down very close to us, and Jessaloup, shaking his hair out of his eyes, snapped his jaw at it — the way he would have if a bird came and bothered us while we were group-feeding, gulping down herring in the icy seas. I shook myself. A hand that wasn't a hand but a fin was the least of my worries. I *had* to civilize him!

"OK — first we've got to get you to walk. I'll show you. OK?"

Again he nodded his head, more slowly this time.

"Look at me. I'm getting up now."

I brought my heels in close, planted my hands in the sand on either side of me, and pushed myself up slowly, first in a crouch, to find my balance, then unfolding myself until I was standing upright. "Do you think you can do that?" I asked. I walked around behind him, and as he bent his knees and brought in his legs, I wrapped my arms through his armpits and around his chest. "Here, I'll help you up. One — two — three!"

One heave, and he was on his feet. I kept my hands on his back, though, because I could feel him teetering backwards.

"No — wait — you've got to find your center of gravity. Not too far back, and not too far forward. Feel it?"

Jessaloup swayed, then steadied himself. Frowning, he nodded.

"OK…" Slowly I withdrew my arms, and moved around

to face him, taking hold of his hands. "Now, try and take a step. Pick up your leg…"

He lifted his right leg, and nearly keeled over sideways. "Steady!" I murmured. He recovered, and put his leg down in front. "That's it," I said, "and now the other one." He took another step. "Perfect!" I encouraged him, walking backwards and pulling him along. "See? You're walking!"

I saw him frown and realized I was talking to him as if he was a little baby. But I couldn't help feeling proud of him. He was taking his first steps, after all…

He pulled his hands free, and pushed me aside. Slowly, with exaggerated care, he lurched forward, his hands stretched out in front, lifting his knees unnecessarily high in the air. "You're getting it!" I laughed. "You're really getting it!" He looked like Frankenstein's monster, swaying from side to side like that, but I didn't tell him. I decided to save it for later, when it would be OK for us to tease each other the way we used to. I could tell he was a bit touchy right now. It couldn't be much fun for him, having to take direction from me, the clueless girl-whale he used to call "Hump," who three years ago had to be taught every little thing — how to dive, where to find the best krill and how to gather up your strength to leap clear of the waves.

ten

AFTER about ten minutes of staggering up and down the beach, Jessaloup was beginning to get the hang of it, and his walking began to look more normal, his arms swinging by his side like mine. Then I showed him how to run, which was a whole new set of moves, something I'd never really thought about before — how you have to bend your knees and push off hard with the ball of your foot to get yourself going. After one false start and falling flat on his face, he began to get it. It wasn't long before he was able to keep up with me.

"All right," I panted, plopping down on the sand. "Let's rest." He sat down with a surprised look on his face, pointing to his open mouth, then at mine. I laughed. "Yeah, we're breathing hard," I explained, "because we've been running. When you're human, you run out of breath much faster than when you're a whale." I took a deep, exaggerated breath, and he did the same. "Our lungs are smaller, I guess." We sat there panting self-consciously for a while, slowly getting our breath back.

"Now," I said, "you have to learn how to talk human. It's a bit different from whale talk. Look. Watch me. The sound comes from up here, in your throat." I took his hand and placed it against my throat. His fingers felt cool to my skin. I started getting this squirmy feeling…

Concentrate, Isabel!

"Aaaa…" I said. "Feel it?"

Nodding slowly, he put his hand against his own throat and opened his mouth. "Aaarrr.." he said.

"Great!" I said.

"Aaarrhhh!" he rattled. "Rrraaarrhh!"

"OK," I giggled, "that's good, but if you want to be understood, you have to learn to make different sounds, to form words."

He frowned at me, then opened his mouth again. "Ehhhrrr…" he said solemnly.

It's harder than you think, teaching someone to talk. Especially if you haven't ever really given it any thought before. I suppose I did learn to talk once, but it was so long ago that I can't remember how I did it. At least I didn't have to teach him the sense of the words, since he seemed to understand everything I said. He just didn't know how to make the sounds. First I taught him the vowels — a, e, i, o and u. He was good at those, and quickly got the hang of them. Then I showed him how to use his tongue, the roof of his mouth and his lips to form the hard, soft or clipped sounds — the consonants. Those were harder for him to master.

"Buh," I prompted him. "Ccc. Duh…. Now you."

He nodded and repeated the sounds. We went through the whole alphabet that way, with only a couple of mishaps. "Don't spit!" I laughed, wiping my face. Then I showed him how to string the sounds together to form the words. "Water," I said. "Waves. Whale. Beach. Sand."

For a few seconds he was silent, as if thinking it over. Then he opened his mouth experimentally.

"Iz-zabel," he said.

It was his very first word.

eleven

TEACHING Jessaloup to walk and talk had taken up the whole afternoon, and I suddenly realized that the sun was low in the sky.

"It's getting late," I said anxiously. "I've got to think about getting home."

He looked at me quizzically. "Home?"

"Where I live," I explained quickly. The word "home" means something quite different in whale-speech, of course. To the whales it's the place they migrate to once a year, down south, in the tropics, where they go to relax and choose a mate, and where they have their babies. "With my family. My pod. In a — house." I pointed to the roofline of a group of oceanfront houses in the distance. "Like one of those." When I had been a whale, Jessaloup and his cousins had been curious about our way of life here on land, and I'd learned that it isn't easy to describe the stuff you've always taken for granted, like living in a house, watching TV or needing money to pay for things you want to buy.

"House," he said. "Home?"

"Yes," I explained, "Home is inside a house."

"Why?" he said. "Why" was one of the first words I'd taught him, and he was making good use of it.

"Because — that's where we live," I said lamely. "And also," I realized, "it's to keep us safe from... from wild animals and bugs, and burglars and storms, and..." *OMG.* I jumped to my feet, slapping the sand off my legs. "We've got to find you a place to spend the night, Jessaloup!"

"*Why?*" he said, patting the sand on either side of him.

"No, no, not here! You can't stay here, you're human now, you'll be miserable if you stay out here all night long without a tent or a sleeping bag or anything! And what if some cop came and asked you what you were doing—"

He pointed at the water with his flipper. "Then *there.*"

"You can't sleep in the sea, you'll drown! And besides, without your whale-blubber, it'll be much too cold for you tonight. Believe me, you won't like it. It won't feel the way you're used to. You'll freeze. You can die of hypothermia." My mind was bouncing around inside my skull, thinking of all the possibilities. Take him home with me? No, I couldn't do that, not now — not yet. How was I going to explain it if I brought home a total stranger with a deformed hand who could barely speak English? What would I tell them if they asked me where he was from, what he was doing here? A motel? No — I didn't have a credit card, where would I get the money? And besides, wouldn't it look suspicious, a kid all by himself, without any luggage?

It was going to take some time to work it all out, and to make Jessaloup a bit more… presentable. Polish him up a bit. The fact was, he was still a little too rough around the edges, a little too weird. There was a whole lot more I was going to have to teach him about acting like a real boy before I could present him to my family or anyone else.

I suddenly remembered the abandoned fisherman's shack down by the old wharf, where my dad kept his old lobster boat. "Come on!" I said. "I know where you can spend the night. Let's go!" I grabbed his hand and pulled him up, flinging my backpack over my shoulder. Stumbling up the beach hand in hand, I felt excited, but also scared. *What* had I got myself into? And yet my dream had come true… seeing Jessaloup again — wasn't that what I'd been wishing for, ever since I had left my ocean life and gone back to living on land? But never in my wildest dreams had I ever imagined *this* — that Jessaloup would come here, beach himself and turn into a boy!

I peeked sideways at him. He was frowning, concentrating on putting one foot in front of the other in the spongy sand. Did he still like me? Or was I being too bossy, was it too hard for him, being human; was he disappointed, did he wish he had never left the ocean?

Why had he come?

We reached the parking lot. I heaved my bike up on its wheels, and steadied it. "Hop on the back," I instructed him, patting the luggage rack.

"Hop? Why?" he said.

I sighed. "Because," I said. "Look," I said, stepping off the bike and showing him how to plant his butt firmly on the luggage rack. "Now you."

He did as I said, and we wobbled off, me pedaling like mad to stay on the road – he was heavy, and it wasn't until he'd finally figured out how to wrap his arms around my waist and cling on tight that we stopped swerving dangerously from side to side.

But it felt great, his arms around my middle and his chin resting on the top of my head.

twelve

IT was close to six o'clock when we reached the fisherman's hut, after the hardest bike ride of my life. Even though I tried to get him to sit still, Jessaloup kept swiveling his head and shoulders from side to side, making the bike weave and lurch all over the road. He had so much to look at — the cars, the buildings, the road signs were all new to him. I did my best to explain each one in turn: "That's a grocery store, where you buy — I mean we catch our food, that's a rose bush, those are flowers, yes, they do smell nice, but... oh that, that's just a dumpster, for garbage, stuff no one wants, I'll explain another time; that's our school, and the soccer field, that's the Pilgrim Tower..."

"Tower!" he exclaimed, looking up. "Home?"

"No, not home, no one lives there. It's just the tallest building in our town. It's, like, you know, 250 feet high," I said proudly. "It's all made of granite. You can climb all the way to the top." The Pilgrim Monument was built a hundred years ago to commemorate the first landing of the Mayflower in 1620, but I decided not to go into that now. If I had to explain about the pilgrims and the Mayflower and Christopher Columbus to Jessaloup, we'd be here all day.

The fisherman's hut looked pretty small and shabby by comparison. When I was little we kids used to come here and play, but I hadn't been here in a long time. My dad's old lobster boat, the *Clorinda*, was looking very sad and abandoned, listing on its lopsided blocks in the weedy lot behind the hut. The rust stains oozing down the sides of the hull made the old tub look like it was weeping. And no wonder: it had been sitting there unused, high and dry, for as long as I could remember.

I couldn't get the door of the shack open at first — it was sagging on its hinges and the bottom was stuck on the floor — but then Jessaloup gave it a big heave with his shoulder, and it swung open with a screech. The hut stank of rancid lobster bait and stale cigarettes, but Jessaloup didn't seem to mind. He gazed around, looking at everything — the two rickety chairs, the pot-bellied stove, the plastic broom in the corner and the dusty, cracked windowpanes.

"Home!" he said cheerfully.

"Yes, but—" I said quickly, not wanting him to think

that this was the way people normally lived, "it's just for tonight. This is kind of crummy. Wait till you see *my* house, it's much nicer than this…"

He wasn't listening. He had spotted a stack of lobster traps in the corner, and an old nylon net hanging on a nail above them. He stared at them in alarm.

"Don't worry," I told him, lifting the net off the nail. "See? It can't hurt you." To Jessaloup's dismay, I wrapped the blue nylon web around my shoulders like a cloak, then shrugged it off and kicked it into a corner. "In the ocean, those things are dangerous," I explained. "But here on land, nets are harmless. See? They won't make you drown."

"Huh," he grunted, nodding. Following my example, he gave it a kick, then stomped on it for good measure.

He sat down on the floor, crossing his legs. He found a cigarette butt next to him, picked it up and stuck it experimentally into his mouth, as if he was going to eat it.

"No! That's dirty!" I yelled, and he spat it out. He gazed at me mournfully.

It suddenly occurred to me he must be hungry. "Have you eaten anything today?" I asked. He looked at me, then looked down at his stomach, puzzled.

I started fumbling in my backpack. Had I brought my wallet? Thank God, I had, and there was some money in there. Oh, and there was my MP3 player; I pulled it out as well. "Here," I said, sticking an earbud into Jessaloup's ear, "you can listen to this while I go find you something to eat."

When I saw him starting to bop his head to the music, I suddenly knew everything was going to be all right.

"Stay here, Jessaloup," I said, "OK? I'll be back soon."

He looked at me, and for the first time since he had become human, a wide smile spread over his face. His even teeth were dazzling white. "OK," he said, drumming his flipper on his knees.

thirteen

I RACED to the Snack Shack in a daze. What had happened, exactly? I hadn't yet had a minute to think it through. Jessaloup had beached himself, turned into a human... But he hadn't told me why. And I hadn't yet asked him anything either. I was dying to know how the rest of my whale family was, especially Mistenbel, the adorable baby whale I had seen being born, who must have grown quite a bit since I had last seen her. And what about the others — Onijonah, who was Mistenbel's mother and my guardian, or Momboduno, the oldest male in our pod, or my little friends Delight and Tomturan, or our whole crazy gang — Dilgruel and Trog, Bickseye and Lemmertail?

At the take-out, I stood staring at the menu for a good minute, even though I knew it by heart. What kind of food would a boy-whale like?

"Uh… One order of fried clams, please," I told Jim, the owner.

"One order of fried clams coming up!" Jim said. "You've started to like clams now, eh, young lady? See, I told you they're the best!"

"Better give me a large fries too," I said. "And a Coke."

When I returned to the fisherman's shack with the food, Jessaloup jumped to his feet. I had to snatch the fries out of his hands before he choked to death on them — he'd thrown his head back and had started pouring them down his throat. "Look," I said, showing him how to chew them one at a time, "this is the way you do it."

"OK," he said, grabbing the paper bag from me and stuffing his mouth by the handful. "Good," he said, chewing happily, his mouth wide open. Bits of fried clam came spilling out.

"That's disgusting!" I scolded him. "Close your mouth when you eat!"

Next I had to show him how to drink from the can without pouring it all over his face. He quickly got the idea, and chugged it down loudly like a baby drinking from a bottle.

"Listen," I told him, making him sit down in a corner away from the broken window. "I've got to get back to my house. If I don't show up for dinner they'll call the police."

"P-lice?" he asked.

"I'll explain another time. You stay in here and get some sleep. Understand? Don't go anywhere!"

"Don't go anywhere," he agreed.

"I'll be back first thing in the morning," I said. "Good night, Jessaloup."

"Gnight, Hump," he said.

fourteen

At home they were furious. "Where have you been?" my mother shrieked at me. "I sent Jacob back to the beach to look for you!"

"Oh," I said. "Sorry. I must have just missed him."

"You *know* how your mother worries — couldn't you have called to tell us where you were? Really, babe!" said my dad.

"I went for a swim, and then I guess I forgot the time."

"You went for a *swim*?" my father roared. "How many times do we have to tell you we don't want you going in the ocean? What were you thinking? Really, Isabel!"

"I don't know…" I stammered. Dad was even more of a worrier than Mom. I just didn't get why he so hated me going near the water — after all, he used to make a living from the sea; he'd been a lobsterman before I was born. I had often begged him to take me out in his old boat, which had been rotting there behind the old wharf for as long as I could remember. But Dad wouldn't hear of it. He was so grouchy about it. He would say that his fishing days were over, and then he would change the subject.

My grandmother, who was staying with us, came shuffling into the room. "She's back?" she asked in her quavery voice. "See now, no need to worry. I *told* you."

"Sorry, Mom, sorry, Dad, sorry Gram. I left my phone at home." This was true, but to be honest, I hadn't thought about calling home. I'd been too busy thinking about Jessaloup. Like, how long would it take to knock him into some kind of shape so that I could introduce him to the family? Why hadn't I found the courage to ask him what he was doing here? Why had I been so tongue-tied? What had been holding me back?

"You know that we're supposed to be leaving tomorrow afternoon, for the Sherwoods's wedding," said Dad, who had already simmered down. He could never stay mad at me long. "But now I don't know — Can we really leave you in charge, babe? We're relying on you to take care of Gram and her cats. Can we really trust you not to…"

"Don't be silly, Dad," I sighed. "Of course you can trust me. You *know* I'm responsible. I just forgot to call, that's all. It won't happen again, I promise."

When Jacob returned from driving around looking for me and saw me sprawled in front of the TV, he picked up a couch cushion and threw it at my head.

"Jeez, Izz, I'm fed up with being your babysitter! Can't you *try* to act like a normal person? You got Mom and Dad all freaked out, and of course then *I* have to go out looking for you. You do it on purpose, don't you, you little jerk!"

In my family, if you ever dared to do something wrong just once, they immediately acted as if you were *always* doing it. They acted as if it was part of your makeup, a horrible flaw in your character. It wasn't fair. It wasn't as if I'd ever stayed out late before without letting them know where I was.

Except that one time — the time I went on a whale watch, and stayed away a whole year.

So to be fair, I couldn't really blame them.

I guess.

fifteen

I GOT up very early the next morning, and left a note on the kitchen table wishing my parents a good trip. It said that I had my phone with me, and I'd gone out to collect signatures for my Kids-For-Whales petition.

Kids-For-Whales was the club I had started to raise awareness about the many dangers threatening marine mammals. Our latest petition was to pressure Washington to pass a bill that would stop the Navy from broadcasting loud noises underwater as part of its naval exercises. Marine biologists were worried that the sound — high-intensity sonar — would cause serious harm to the whales and other sea creatures, and from my own experience I knew that they were definitely on to something. The whales had taught me to find my way around the ocean by listening for my own calls bouncing back to me off distant objects, a trick they called "ringing and pinging" (scientists call it *echo-location*.) In the ocean, sound carries for many miles. If you ran into loud noises, and couldn't hear yourself ringing or pinging, you could easily get confused, or lost. You risked crashing into rocks or colliding with a ship; you could even get yourself stranded on a beach somewhere by accident.

I had packed a bag with some clothes from my oldest brother Alex's closet — I figured he wouldn't mind, since he was away at college — plus a sleeping bag, a flashlight, an Ace bandage and a couple of bran muffins I'd found in the kitchen.

"Jessaloup!" I whispered through the door when I arrived at the fisherman's shack. "Wake up! It's me, Isabel!"

There was no sign of life from inside. Cautiously I pushed the door open.

The hut was deserted.

I spun around, panicked. Where had he gone? Had he wandered off and lost his way? Had someone found him, and called the police? Was he in custody somewhere, had they noticed his flipper-hand, did they think he was an alien — An *alien*! OMG, what if they locked him up and had scientists perform experiments on him? I peered at the ocean, my head in an uproar. Stupid, stupid! I should never have left him alone... Now I'd never know what had brought him here. I'd never know if... What an idiot I'd been, to leave him by himself all night!

Just then I spotted a swimmer, way out beyond the surf. A very strong swimmer, splashing merrily in the waves.

Jessaloup?

He caught sight of me standing on the beach, and waved enthusiastically. Seconds later he caught a wave and bodysurfed elegantly all the way up onto the beach.

"Hey, Hump," he panted, coughing some seawater out of his lungs.

"I thought you promised not to call me that any more," I pouted. When I'd first become a member of the pod, "Hump" had been Jessaloup's nickname for me after I committed the blunder of calling our species of whale "humpbacks" instead of "Sirens,"— the Singing Ones.

Fortunately I'd thought of bringing a towel, which I wrapped around him, since he was shivering. He had goose bumps all over and his lips were blue. "How long have you been in the water?" I scolded him.

He shrugged, and pointed to the sun, then drew an arc with his finger down to the horizon.

"Since the sun came up? You've been in the water for, like, four hours! You're human now! The sea is too cold to stay in that long!"

He made a face, then tugged at my hand. "Come on," he said.

"No, not now, Jessaloup! I'll come for a swim later, maybe, but first you have to have some breakfast. Look, I've brought you some clothes."

Back at the fishing shack I had to show him how to peel the pleated paper off the muffin before stuffing it into his mouth and gulping it down. Then I took out the Ace bandage.

"Look, I'm going to wrap this thing around your flipper," I showed him, "to hide it." I wrapped the bandage in a figure eight, the way I'd been shown in First Aid class, securing it with two elastic clips.

He stared down at it.

"Is it too tight? No? Can you still move it?"

He made a fist, experimentally. "That's good," I said. "Now it just looks as if you've hurt your hand."

I made him get dressed in my brother's clothes, and I must say that in a Red Sox jersey, Alex's swimming trunks and a pair of flip-flops on his feet, he looked almost normal.

"OK now, talk to me," I said, when he was finished eating. We were sitting on the jetty, our feet dangling down. "Have you been practicing talking?"

"Yess," he said.

"*Yes,*" I corrected him. "Make the S at the end a little softer, like this, see?"

He nodded. "Yezz. Izzabel. That better?"

"Much better," I said.

"Talking human izzn't hard," he said confidently. "Onezz you get the hang of it."

"You're doing very well," I said.

"Been listening to your song box," he said, pointing to my iPod. "Good songs. Catch a wave. Let it rock. Walkin-on-sunshine. In an octopuzz's garden in the shade. Love sick."

"Lovesick!" I laughed. "Do you even know what that means?"

He was looking at me strangely.

"Well anyway, that's good," I said quickly. My heart was beating faster. I felt myself turning red.

In the ocean it had taken me a while (don't ask me why I'd been so dense!), but I had finally found out that when a male Siren wants to woo a female, he does it by singing her his very special Siren Song — the most romantic, glorious serenade in the whole world.

But I had also found out, to my great embarrassment, that Jessaloup wasn't allowed to sing to me. Even if he'd wanted to. The whales had decided that since I was destined to return to the human world, I was not to be wooed or sung to. The risk was too great: the ocean might then claim me forever.

And now? It was time to ask him the questions — so many questions! — that I was dying to know. But the only one I could think of right now was:

Was he here just because of *me*?

sixteen

I CLEARED my throat, but I couldn't think of what to say next. How to begin. My throat felt thick and dry. My head was in a whirl. Why was it so hard? When we'd been two whales in the ocean, we had understood each other. There hadn't been any awkwardness between us. But now...

It was Jessaloup who went first. Or tried to, anyway. "Isabel," he said. "I have to tell you..." Apparently he could still read my mind. I held my breath. He swallowed, then started again. "I came to dry-land, because..."

He was interrupted by a shout from the boardwalk. I looked up, and saw Tom. My ex-boyfriend, waving at me. My heart sank with a crash. He came running up to where we were sitting. What you'd call really bad timing. Really! I was *really* not in the mood to see Tom just then.

"I've been looking for you everywhere," Tom panted, flipping a hank of blond hair out of his eyes. "Your mother told me you had gone out to collect signatures — Why didn't you call me...?"

Tom was supposed to be the Vice President of the Kids-For-Whales Club. He had been enthusiastic at first, but this year he'd lost interest in it, which was one of the reasons we'd broken up. Guiltily, I remembered that I had promised to come listen to his band if he'd help me collect signatures.

"Hey, Tom," I said, trying to be nonchalant. "I — I just happened to bump into an old friend." I turned to Jessaloup, who was scowling dangerously at Tom. "Tom, meet, uh, my friend Jesse. Jesse — this is Tom."

"Hey, Jesse," said Tom. "Whassup."

Jessaloup, who had raised his eyebrows at being called 'Jesse,' grunted, "Hey."

"Has she got you roped in as well, dude?" Tom asked.

Jessaloup looked at me, puzzled.

"You know, to help her save her precious whales," Tom explained.

Jessaloup stared at him. "Save the whales?" he gaped.

"He doesn't know what you're talking about," I told Tom hastily. "He only just, you know, got here, and..."

"Really," Tom said. He put his hand on the nape of my neck, under my hair, and gave it a proprietary squeeze. I sensed Jessaloup going rigid beside me. "So where did you two meet?"

"Oh, um, you know, at sleep-away camp, two summers ago," I lied. "He's just — visiting."

"Well, anyway, I just came to tell you where we're jamming today. Final rehearsal. In Jordan's garage. The Battle of the Bands is tomorrow, so we're practicing all day. You *are* coming, aren't you?"

I nodded my head. "Yeah, sure. But not right now."

"You have to come," he insisted. "We've got this *sick* new song. I'm sure we're going to win. I really want you to hear it. Dillon's borrowed his cousin's new amp. I tell you, it's sick, man."

"*Sick?*" said Jessaloup. "*Song?*"

Tom nodded. "Yeah." Turning his back on Jessaloup, he said, "Bring the dude too if you have to. C'mon, we're rehearsing it right now."

I shrugged. "Maybe later, OK?"

"It's a great song. I wrote it. You've *got* to come hear us practice it."

"I'm sure it's great," I said, squinting as if something really interesting way out at sea had caught my eye.

"Whatever," he said awkwardly. He started walking away backwards. "Later. Right?"

"Later!" I muttered. I went on peering into the distance. I was feeling guilty as hell.

We sat there for a minute or so, not speaking. Suddenly Jessaloup got up and vaulted down on to the sand.

"Wait!" I yelled. "Jessaloup!"

He stopped at the water's edge, but didn't turn around.

I was out of breath when I reached his side. "Aren't you

going to finish telling me what you were going to say?" I asked.

He refused to look at me. *"Jesse?"* he muttered. "What's wrong with Jessaloup?"

"Nothing's wrong with your name!" I said quickly. "Your name is great. It's an awesome name. Only – I thought you'd fit in better, you know, with a name that people have heard of. I mean — here on land," I went on nervously. "It's shorter, anyway," I added, lamely. I had forgotten that the whales prided themselves on their long names. The more musical, the better.

"Like 'Tom' is shorter," he snorted.

"Not like Tom," I said defensively. "That's got nothing to do with it."

Jessaloup shook his dreadlocks. He took a breath, then didn't say anything.

I racked my brain for something I could say that would lighten the mood, to change the subject. But Jessaloup went first.

"So, how sick is he?" he asked.

"Who, Tom? No, he's not sick! Did he look sick to you?"

"He said, 'It's sick.'"

"Oh, I see. No, he was talking about his song…" I had to laugh. "Sometimes we use words that are the opposite of what we really mean. It's a kind of slang. He meant it's cool, it's great." There was so much I still had to explain to him! I didn't even know where to start. "Like…" I tried to think of another example. "Like, if I thought you were really stupid, you know, I might say, 'Genius!' But you're supposed to get that I meant the opposite."

"How?"

"It's the way I say it. It's sarcastic. Like — when you call me 'Hump,' I know you don't really mean I look like a hump. You're just teasing. Get it?"

He kicked a clamshell into the water. We both stared at it as it twirled down to the shallow bottom. There was another awkward silence.

"So anyway," I finally said, "you were going to tell me why you came." My heart was beating very fast. "How come you beached yourself."

He didn't answer. I had the feeling he wasn't really listening. His mind was on something else. I tugged on his arm.

"I mean," I persisted, "I thought only humans, like me, you know, the Chosen Ones, could do it, could change into a whale. Now it seems you can do the same thing, the other way around. What's up with that?"

What I really wanted to say was — If he could do it, why had he waited so long?

"We can do it too," he said dully.

"Well *duh*. But — how?"

"You have to be sent. And you're only ever sent if there is a really good reason for it," he said.

"O—K?" I said. My heart was starting to beat even faster.

"A really, *really* good reason." He stopped.

"So — then what was the reason for sending you?" I

said, trying my best to control my breathing.

He finally raised his head. He looked at me mournfully.

"Tell me!" I insisted.

He picked up a stone, and flung it violently into the sea.

"Danger," he said.

seventeen

DANGER?

It was so different from what I'd been expecting him to say that it felt as if I had been slapped in the face. My cheeks were burning. I stared at him open-mouthed. "What do you mean, danger?" I squeaked.

He sighed. "I am the messenger. I was sent. To warn the humans."

"Warn us! What about?"

"A big danger. The biggest wave."

"The biggest wave?" I shook my head. I couldn't get my head around this. What was he talking about?

"The big wave will drown the dry land," he said.

Was he kidding — a *tidal wave?*

"I was sent. To find you. And warn you."

"Sent by *who?*" I demanded. Although I already knew the answer.

"You know. The elders. Indigoneah, Momboduno, Bonahdiboh. They told me to find you. Isabel will know what to do, they said."

I was so crushed to hear that it wasn't Jessaloup's own idea to come and find me that I was having a hard time focusing on what he was actually telling me. I started tugging at my hair. It's a habit I have when I'm trying to think. "How do they know?"

"It's in the Song," Jessaloup said. "*Everyone* knows. All the whales know."

"OK, so when is this thing supposed to happen?" I snapped. He's got to be pulling my leg, I thought. "Today? How come you didn't say so before?"

"Not today. But soon."

"*How soon?*"

"Nineteen moonlights before the longest day."

The longest day, the longest day? The — "You mean the solstice?" I tried to remember what we had learned in seventh grade — the longest day of the year, and the shortest night. Midsummer's day. June 21st, wasn't it? And today was May 31st. "Wait a second. Nineteen nighttimes before…" I did a quick calculation in my head. "But that's tomorrow! You mean there's actually going to be a big wave, *here*, like, tomorrow night?"

Jessaloup nodded glumly. "After the sun drops into the

sea. The Song tells it. The ocean floor will shake, and the big wave will rise up. Here, in this part of the ocean."

It felt like a punch to the stomach. It took me a few moments to get my breath back.

"If that's true, why didn't you tell me right from the start?" I cried, indignant. "I mean, we wasted nearly a whole day…"

"Didn't have the words," he said simply. "I had to learn human talk first."

I was boiling mad. I wanted to punch something. "But then why didn't you come sooner?"

"They sent me as soon as it was known, as soon as the Song told it. We were in the cold waters. It took me six daylights to swim here. Everyone else has to stay clear of the coast. The big wave is very dangerous; you can get smashed against the shore if you're not careful."

If this was true, it was finally beginning to dawn on me, this could be the greatest disaster of my lifetime. A tsunami crashing on to the East Coast of the USA, flattening everything in its way… Thousands, no, *millions* of people and animals might be swept out to sea and drowned — and Jessaloup and I were the only humans who knew about it!

This couldn't be happening!

I sank to my knees, because my legs were suddenly shaking so badly that they wouldn't hold me up.

"What do they expect *me* to do about it?" I gasped. "I'm just a girl. Who's going to listen to me?"

"Not just you. You and me," he said. "Us."

eighteen

I DIDN'T know what to do. I was freaking out. I was a basket case. But I tried to pull myself together. *Isabel will know what to do* — The whales were counting on me. I couldn't let them down!

I made Jessaloup keep out of sight, in the fisherman's hut. I'd decided that if we bumped into anyone else, we'd say that his last name was Jonah. Jesse Jonah, that sounded about right to me. Jessaloup still wasn't too happy about the name change, I could tell, but to my relief he didn't make a fuss about it. The story was that he was a friend from camp, that he had come all the way from Canada on a surprise visit. From French-speaking Quebec. That would explain his accent, because his English still sounded a little strange. I was amazed at how much his speech and his manners had improved in less than a day, but I didn't think he was quite ready yet to be presented to the world. I couldn't deal with having to explain his weirdness just now. I had more important things to do. I told him to wait in the hut until I returned.

Meanwhile, the clock was ticking. If Jessaloup was right, the tsunami would hit tomorrow night. I had to tell the police. Or the Coast Guard. Or Homeland Security. Or whoever was in charge. There would have to be a mass evacuation, wouldn't there? But didn't those things take time? OMG! OMG! OMG! There was no time to waste!

I raced home, but my parents' car was no longer parked out front. They had already left for the wedding. Just as well, I decided — they'd be out of harm's way, high and dry in the Adirondack mountains. At least I didn't have to worry about *them*.

I jumped back on my bike and headed for the Police Station a few blocks down the road. I tried to compose myself as I walked up to the desk. I was a bit out of breath. "Can I please see the Chief?" I asked.

The officer at the desk didn't look up.

"Can I please see the Chief?" I said again.

The officer continued to ignore me. He made me wait until he'd finished filling out some form. I just stood there turning red, feeling like a fool. At last he turned to me, ever so slowly, and said, "How can I help?"

"I need to speak to the Chief," I told him.

"Oh you do, do you? What do you want with the Chief?" he asked, teasing.

"It's urgent," I said.

"Oh, urgent, is it!" he said benevolently. "It always is, isn't it. Shoot. You can tell me first."

"I — I have to warn the authorities that there's going to be a tsunami," I said. I was mortified to feel myself getting red. I hoped he couldn't tell how nervous I was.

"Ho!" he said with a wink. "Well. Never heard *that* one before!" He leered at me, waggling his eyebrows. "But I don't think we should disturb the Chief, do you? Oh, I know — school's almost over. It's the last week before summer break, isn't it? Bunch of juvenile delinquents, you kids." He started to get up from his desk, slowly. I shrank back a bit, uncertain. "It never fails," he went on. "Don't think we aren't ready for your practical jokes. Prank week! I got one of you hell-raisers at home myself. Jimmy Brummon. Is he a friend of yours? Did that little punk put you up to this?"

I shook my head. "No, but you see…"

"You don't want to get the Chief mad. He gets mad easily," said the officer in his deep voice, rattling the keys on his belt. "He might even have you locked up for spreading false rumors. Wouldn't want that, would we? I think you'd better go home now. Run along. I'm doing you a favor."

I stood there dithering, not knowing what to do.

"Go on, scram. Before *I* get mad. Out."

Five seconds later I was out on the sidewalk. I wanted to kick myself for not being braver. I was glad Jessaloup hadn't been there to see me cave like that. But it's hard to stand up for yourself when you know that the story you're telling is too far-out for words.

I took a deep breath, and looked up the street. Town Hall — I'd try the Mayor next. This time I wouldn't take no for an answer.

My knees still felt weak, so I walked my bike to Town Hall. Leaning it against the railing by the front stoop, I went in. The lady at the desk asked how she could help.

"I'd like to speak to the Mayor," I said.

"We don't have a mayor, dear," she said. "What is it about? You probably want the Town Manager."

"All right," I said. "Can I see the Town Manager?"

"He's not in his office right now," she said, peering at me over the top of her reading glasses. "He only has office hours Wednesdays and Thursdays. Eight to twelve."

I sighed. "So who else is there I can speak to?"

"It depends what this is about," she said.

"It's very important," I said. "I can't tell you."

I could tell, from her *isn't-this-cute?* expression, that she wasn't taking me seriously. "Let's see — You can leave a request in writing to go before the Town Selectmen. Their next meeting is July18."

As I stormed out, I heard her call after me, "Try again tomorrow. The Town Clerk will be in then!"

This was a joke, a horrible, horrible joke. No adult was going to believe me. I had no proof, and if I told them the real story, they'd think I was spaced out on drugs or something. Or, worse, they'd send me to the funny farm.

Unless…

Mr. Peake.

Yes, what about Mr. Peake?

The only grownup I could think of who might — just *might* — hear me out was Mr. Peake, my fifth-grade teacher, the one who had taken us on the whale watch three years ago. Mr. Peake now taught Chemistry and Biology at the High School. I knew he had always felt responsible for my disappearance, and I didn't think he'd ever believed the story I had invented — that after falling into the sea, I was washed up on a desert island. He was a scientist, and scientists aren't fooled that easily.

But how could I persuade him that I wasn't fooling him now?

nineteen

FORTUNATELY Mr. Peake hadn't left school yet. He looked up from his desk when I pushed open the door of the science lab and stepped inside.

"Isabel!" he said, smiling warmly.

"Are you busy?" I asked.

"Never too busy to talk to you, Miss. Pull up a stool. So — how's things?"

I climbed on one of the stools at the first lab bench, sighed, and looked down at my hands. "I've got a problem," I said.

"Is it your school work? Do you need extra help?"

I shook my head. "That isn't it. A *big* problem."

"I see. Well, I'm usually a big solver of little problems. Big problems — I'm not so sure." He grinned. "But try me."

I looked out the window. The light was clear and sharp, the sky as blue as in a postcard. A thin wisp of cloud came drifting into view from the left side of the window frame. It meandered over to the Pilgrim Tower, and disappeared behind it. I waited for it to straggle out again on the other side before saying, "You never really believed my story, did you, about what happened to me?"

"No, not really." He was staring at me, eyebrows raised. "Are you going to come clean, then? I should say it's about time."

"I didn't think anyone would believe me," I said.

"I never believed you anyway. So you might as well fess up. Give me the *real* story."

"I've never told anyone," I said. "It's hard."

He didn't say anything, but continued to gaze at me expectantly.

"Uh —," I said, "ummm—"

"Go on," he said. "I'm listening."

I looked up at a flickering ceiling light overhead. "Er, well, would you believe me if I told you that when I fell overboard, I turned into a whale?"

At that, he sat up and laughed. "Really?" he said.

"Really," I said, when he was done laughing. "See? I *knew* you wouldn't believe it."

"Don't go jumping to conclusions. Miss. *I'll* tell you if I believe it or not." He rattled his pen on his desk.

"However, you had better do an *extremely* good job of explaining it, because that's quite a tale you're giving me here to swallow."

I decided I'd better not look at him, so that if there was scorn or disbelief written all over his face, I wouldn't see it and lose my nerve. I stared down at my knees, took a deep breath, and then I just went for it. It all came pouring out – how surprised I had been to find myself able to stay underwater, comfortably floating way down below the surface, how the water hadn't felt at all cold, how it had taken me several minutes to realize I seemed to have blown up into this enormous creature, how incredibly weird that was, how the whales had been expecting me, how they had come from near and far to greet me —

"Aha," Mr. Peake interrupted me. "I did always wonder about that, you know. Never could explain it — all those whales appearing out of nowhere, suddenly flocking around our boat. Hundreds of them! That was something, wasn't it? Incredible! Numbers like that, the diversity of the species — it's never been seen before, or since, to my knowledge. I asked several experts, but they had never heard of anything like it. It was truly unique, a unique phenomenon."

I glanced up at Mr. Peake. I couldn't tell if he was mocking me. Or was he in fact taking me seriously? But I couldn't help bristling at his choice of words. "It's *not* a 'phenomenon,' actually," I said. "It's a gathering. It's what the whales do when they are called together to welcome a Chosen One."

"Chosen One?" he asked. "Now what's that?"

"People like me," I said modestly. "I mean that's what the whales call us. Humans who come to them. We're also called mer-humans, or mermen and mermaids."

He looked at me flabbergasted. Then he grinned. "Oh ho, I see!" he said with a wink. "Mermaids! Now I get it. So it's — fairy tales do come true and all that, right?" But when he saw I was serious, he pursed his lips and said, "Sorry, do go on. How many of you mer-humans are there, then? Tell me."

I shrugged. "Oh, it only happens once in a hundred years or so. It's not that common."

"No, I don't suppose that it is," Mr. Peake said.

twenty

IT took a while to tell Mr. Peake everything I could remember about my life with the whales, and I could sense him wavering from skepticism and disbelief to curiosity and respect. And then back again.

"Well," he said finally, "young lady, you astonish me. I think that either you've been studying the life of marine mammals extremely thoroughly, since you appear to know more about them than any marine biologist..."

"But I'm only telling you all that stuff to prove I'm telling the truth," I said, swallowing the lump of disappointment in my throat. Did he really think I'd go to such lengths just to make up some wild story?

"…let me finish. Or else you did indeed have this, er, experience. Incredible as it might seem. Actually, I would like to believe your story, crazy as it is. Nothing else makes sense — your disappearance, your mysterious return home; I knew your story about building that raft wasn't true. Remember when you were asked to build another raft, to show how you'd done it, and you weren't able to? You said you'd forgotten. But you didn't even try."

I felt fifty pounds lighter, suddenly. Was he starting to believe me?

"But," he went on suspiciously, "why tell me *now*? You've been keeping this secret for three whole years. Why wait this long, if you've been wanting to get it off your chest?"

I took a deep breath. "There's something else," I said. "Something that's happening now. Something terrible."

"Oh?"

"Something really, REALLY urgent," I said.

"Well! That sounds serious."

"It is," I said.

"And what would that be?"

I just blurted it out. "There's going to be this huge tsunami tomorrow, and we've got to warn everybody."

"Whoa, whoa, a tsunami?" Mr. Peake almost lost his cool. His eyebrows were raised so high that his eyes seemed to be popping out of his head. "What has that got to do with the whales? What are you telling me?"

"See," I said nervously, "they — the whales — think I'm, uh, more important than I really am. They think I can fix things. That's because I showed them some human tricks when I was a whale, so I guess now they think I can solve any problem…"

Mr. Peake got up from his desk. "This is too much! You mean you've been receiving secret messages from your friends out there, all this time?"

"No, that's not how… I never heard from them, not until yesterday," I said. "I just…"

"But a tsunami! Do you even know what you're saying? We don't have tsunamis here, on the Eastern seaboard! Really, my dear, I don't think…"

"No, no, please, you've got to believe me! There's going to be one here, tomorrow evening, it could be, *will* be a terrible disaster!"

"Listen, Isabel. I'd like to believe you, but this is impossible. How would you possibly know this? I think you are pulling my leg."

I was starting to sweat. "Please, Mr. Peake! I have proof!"

"What sort of proof?"

"Just — come with me. I'll show you. OK?"

twenty-one

I DRAGGED Mr. Peake outside, and started running down the steps.

"Where are we going?" he shouted.

"To the old dock," I shouted back.

"Here, we'll take my van," he said, opening the driver's side door.

I jumped in on the other side. "The old dock," I directed him. "All the way down the end."

Five minutes later, as we pulled up to the dock, we could see Jessaloup sitting outside the fisherman's hut, chewing on a hunk of seaweed. He spat it out when he spotted us. I gestured that it was OK, he didn't have to hide.

"There's my proof," I told Mr. Peake, pointing at him.

"Who? That young man?" he asked, shading his eyes. "Do I know him? What year is he?"

"No, he's not at our school," I said. I gulped, my breath coming fast. "Actually, he's from — the ocean."

"What do you mean, he's from the ocean!"

"He *is*. He's like me, only in reverse. He's a whale, in real life. A humpback."

Mr. Peake was shaking his head. "Isabel, I've had enough. Stop playing me for a fool, will you? It's been fun, but enough's enough."

We had reached the hut. Jessaloup looked up at us innocently.

"Tell him," I said urgently. "Tell this man who you are."

"Uh, Jesse Jonah," said Jessaloup.

"No, silly," I said. "Tell him *what* you are. Go on."

"A boy," he said obediently.

Mr. Peake was tapping his foot.

"No, no!" I shouted at Jessaloup. "Tell the man what you *really, really* are!"

"Really?" asked Jessaloup.

"Yes, really!" I yelled, exasperated.

Mr. Peake was about to turn and leave. "Look!" I shouted at him. I grabbed Jessaloup's left arm and started tearing the bandage off his flipper. "Mr. Peake, look! Here's your proof!"

twenty-two

I HAD never been to Mr. Peake's house before. It was a small gray Cape backing up to the sandy dunes, with a wide porch in front. We had decided to keep Jessaloup's identity a secret, at least for now, since revealing it would only complicate matters. Mr. Peake and I agreed that the most important thing for us to do right now was to sound the alarm about the tsunami.

"If it turns out Jesse's wrong," said Mr. Peake, "we're in major trouble."

"I know," I said. "But we have to take the risk."

Mrs. Peake met us at the door, trying to hold back a barking black Lab. "I'm sorry, I don't know what's come over him," she grunted, yanking on his collar, "he doesn't usually act like this." The dog was straining to get away from her, trying to get at Jessaloup, who didn't seem at all worried at being greeted by an aggressive animal.

"Bunsen, *stay!*" Mr. Peake ordered. "Behave yourself, you silly hound!" At which point Bunsen reared up on his hind legs and slipped his head right out of his collar. Before anyone could stop him he had his paws against Jessaloup's shoulders and was slurping at his face.

"Down, boy!" Mr. Peake yelled. "Down!"

Jessaloup promptly got down on his hands and knees.

"He didn't mean *you!*" I cried. I couldn't help laughing. "He meant the dog!"

But Jessaloup and Bunsen were busy getting acquainted, butting heads and turning around and around each other. I don't think he even heard me.

"Well, come in, come in," said Mrs. Peake. She wore her hair in a short grey pageboy, and a pair of big dangly earrings swung from side to side as she spoke. I decided she and Mr. Peake suited each other. When she was informed that a tsunami might be headed straight for us, I saw her shoot a quizzical glance at her husband, but he just shook his head, as if to say, "Later."

Suddenly I started to feel a little less confident that we'd done the right thing confiding in him. Was he taking us seriously, or was he just pretending? But when Mrs. Peake, tut-tutting, said she was ready to believe anything nowadays, I began to feel a bit better. "Between all that global warming," she said, "and the funny weather we've been having lately, all the rain and the droughts and the forest fires and the hurricanes, nothing would surprise me! It's all those people cranking up their air conditioners when it's perfectly nice out, if you ask me. And leaving their cars running in the parking lot while they're shopping. *So* irresponsible! I don't know *what* those people think they're doing."

Mr. Peake laughed. "My wife is the world's greatest authority on unexplained weather events," he said fondly. "I'm always telling her she ought to be the chairwoman of the Institute of Unconcerned Research."

"He's just joking," I explained to Jessaloup.

"But what we need now is a scientist who can confirm this," he went on. "There won't be an evacuation unless we can offer some pretty persuasive scientific evidence."

"*You're* a scientist, Mr. Peake," I reminded him.

"I appreciate your faith in me, Isabel," he said, "but this is way over my head. I'm just a high-school teacher. I wouldn't know how to lend this credence. We need someone who can investigate, who has the authority to persuade the people in charge that this tsunami is for real. Or not." (Mrs. Peake nodded. Jessaloup scowled.) "An expert. Someone who monitors seismic activity in the oceans and studies earthquakes in earnest. Tsunamis are caused by underwater earthquakes or volcanic eruptions, as you know."

I swallowed. "I don't think you really believe us," I said. "You're just humoring us, aren't you! You don't think it's really going to happen."

"I did not say that, Isabel," he said. "I think that, in light of your — uh, experience with the whales, there may be a valid basis for what Jesse here is saying will happen. I just think we should be careful not to create an unnecessary panic, before we are sure and know exactly what's going on."

"But we *know* what's…" I began.

"I think," he went on calmly, "that we should go to Woods Hole. To the Oceanographic Institution down there. They have all the experts, folks who study everything to do with the oceans. I've been meaning to organize a field trip down there anyway. That's where we are most likely to find someone who can confirm this, one way or another."

"OK then, let's go!" I cried.

"Not now, Isabel." He smiled, and shook his head at me. "It's a two-hour drive. I'm sorry, but it's much too late in the day, they'll be closed by the time we get there. Tell you what. We'll leave first thing in the morning. I promise."

"Tomorrow — but I still have school," I began. My head was spinning. We were running out of time. The clock was ticking. Mr. Peake didn't seem to feel the urgency. Could I trust him? What was I supposed to *do*?

"I'll take care of it. Not to worry. I'll let your teachers know. We'll call it a science research project." He stood up, and, putting his hand on my back, pushed me to the front door. "You go home now, Isabel, and get some sleep. Cheer up, everything will look brighter when you're rested. Just be back here at 6 a.m. pronto. If we leave then, we'll be there when the place opens at 8."

He shooed me out the door with a promise to call my parents on their cell phone and explain he was going to have me help him with a science project over the summer.

"Wait!" I protested, turning back. "What about, I mean…"

"And don't worry. We'll take good care of your friend Jesse," he assured me. "Go now. Nothing bad will happen to him here. He'll be just fine."

twenty-three

A FEW minutes before six the next morning I was back at Mr. Peake's house. My parents, thrilled to hear that I'd found "something educational" to do over the summer, had raised no objections. "As long as you mind your teacher, and don't go running off by yourself, Isabel!" my mother had warned me over the phone.

I had tossed and turned all night, worrying if I'd done the right thing leaving Jessaloup with Mr. and Mrs. Peake. My instincts told me I should trust them, and yet I couldn't help replaying that scene from *E. T.* in my head. You know, when their house is suddenly surrounded by government agents and the extra-terrestrial is whisked into a big white tent and they hook him up to all these wires and monitors. So I can't tell you how relieved I was to see Jessaloup on the front porch, apparently in fine shape, saying goodbye to Bunsen. The two of them were making a spectacle of themselves, rubbing noses and fondly butting heads. I felt a pang of envy.

"I don't know if this is such a good idea," I whispered to Mr. Peake.

"What? Driving down to Woods Hole? Why not?"

"I mean, what if those scientists find out about Jesse being a whale, and…"

Mr. Peake laughed. "Scientists are not the enemy, Isabel. They're not evil, they are here to help, you know. I think you've seen too many science fiction movies."

"Yes, but still," I said.

"We don't need to show them Jesse's fin-hand, if that's what you're worried about. It could complicate matters, you're right. Let's just keep that part between us for now, OK?"

"OK," I said, somewhat relieved.

"Come on, hop in the car," Mr. Peake called out to Jessaloup.

"Car!" said Jessaloup, sticking his head into Mr. Peake's Dodge Caravan. "*Sick!*"

"It's not *sick*," I hissed at him. "It isn't even a car, it's a minivan." I thought he should know the difference.

But Jessaloup paid no attention. He had climbed into the passenger seat and was playing with the buttons on the door, locking and unlocking it, making the window go up and down. I had to show him how to put on the seatbelt, then climbed into the back.

As we drove off, Mr. Peake winked at me in the rear view mirror. "We had quite the night," he said, "didn't we, Jesse?"

Jessaloup grunted. "Meatloaf, Isabel!" he sighed, rubbing his belly. "Carrots!"

"I should have warned you," I started apologizing to Mr. Peake, "he eats a ton…"

Mr. Peake laughed. "My wife was in heaven! He gobbled down most of her meat loaf, half a dozen baked potatoes, a bowlful of carrots and a gallon of ice cream. She said it had been a long time since anyone enjoyed her cooking so much."

Jessaloup was nodding, pleased with himself.

"But I hadn't anticipated that he didn't know about beds," Mr. Peake went on.

"Oh," said Jessaloup. "Sorry I woke you up."

"There was a big bang," Mr. Peake explained to me. "He fell out of bed at two in the morning. I found him on the floor, all tangled up in the sheets."

Jessaloup twisted his head around. "Isabel, humans dream the same as whales!" he said, beaming at me.

I hadn't thought of it before. But it was true: when I'd been a whale, I'd definitely had dreams very much like the ones I had now, even though in the ocean I had never been more than half asleep. When you're in the sea, one part of your brain has to stay awake, so you won't sink and drown.

"So — what was your dream about?" I asked, my heart beating a little faster. I knew what my own dreams were about.

Had Jessaloup been dreaming about me?

He didn't answer.

"Come on, tell me," I pressed him.

"Oh, just…" he said vaguely. "I… Uh, the sea, I guess."

Fine, I fumed silently. Whatever.

"You must miss the sea," Mr. Peake said to him.

"Yes. And no," he said, turning to look at me again.

I avoided his eyes. I gazed out the window at the green dunes zipping past, making myself tuck the disappointment out of the way, somewhere inside. Why couldn't I just be happy to have Jessaloup here with me? Why did I want him to say more?

twenty-four

I MUST have dozed off, because the next thing I knew, we were pulling into the campus of the Oceanographic Institute.

At the desk, the receptionist told us that we were in the wrong building. "You want the Clark Annex," she said, "That's the geology department."

We left the minivan where we'd parked it, and walked up the hill to the Clark Annex.

When Mr. Peake explained what we wanted, we were shown into a big room full of funny looking instruments and cables coiled all over the floor.

"Can I help you?" asked a man in a hooded sweatshirt and jeans.

"Yes, we were hoping to speak to someone about ocean-floor volcanoes and, uh, tsunamis and such," said Mr. Peake. "I'm the science teacher at Provincetown High School."

"Ah, and these two young people are your students?" said the man, shaking hands with us. "You've come to the right place. How-do, I'm Dr. Kreinstead. Always happy to see youngsters expressing an interest in what we do here. I run this lab, so I'm your man. I can show you around, if you like."

As Mr. Peake gushed how good that was of him, I stared at the professor's hoodie. I always thought scientists wore white lab coats and wire-rim glasses.

"The instruments you see here, for instance," — Kreinstead pointed to some bright yellow boxes with rounded corners — "are deep-sea seismometers. They help us to measure earthquake activity on the ocean floor."

"I saw one of these once," Jessaloup told me in a loud whisper. "I didn't know what it was."

"You think you saw one of these, young man?" smiled Dr. Kreinstead. Jessaloup's whisper could be clearly heard: he didn't know yet how to lower the volume of his voice. "That's most unlikely. Unless you've ever dived down to the bottom of the ocean, but I don't think you would be alive today to tell the tale."

I prodded Jessaloup with my elbow, to make him shut up.

Mr. Peake cleared his throat. "What we're interested in, actually, and perhaps you can help us, is whether there is any likelihood of an earthquake setting off a tsunami that could reach the Eastern seaboard."

"Well, I'd say that that was extremely unlikely," said the professor, still smiling.

"But possible?"

"Possible, certainly," he replied. "There is generally a great deal of volcanic activity in the Mid-Atlantic ridge, but it's so deep down that it's barely noticeable here on shore. Would you like me to show you some of our instruments, to see how we monitor what goes on down below?"

He ushered us into a room full of computers and other equipment. A bunch of people who looked like graduate students were gathered around one of the monitors, pointing at something on the screen. They didn't look up when we walked in.

"Hey, Doc," said one of them. "Come look at this."

"Crazy read-outs, overnight," said another, his voice cracking with excitement. "It's going haywire."

"Couldn't it be a malfunction?" asked a girl in a turtleneck, squinting through granny-glasses.

"Let's have a look," said Dr. Kreinstead, moving the others out of the way and planting himself on a chair in front of the monitor. "When did these data come in?"

I looked around the room. Everyone was huddled around Dr. Kreinstead, glued to the screen. I felt the buzz of excitement in the air. I pushed my elbow out to give Jessaloup a meaningful poke.

But my elbow hit nothing – just empty air.

With a shock, I realized Jessaloup was no longer standing next to me. Where had he gone? I took a few cautious steps back, then turned toward the entrance.

Jessaloup was gone. Vanished.

I broke out in a cold sweat — Had someone come tiptoeing up behind us and thrown a hood over his head? Had he been kidnapped without anyone noticing?

No, I scolded myself, of course not, you fool... Surely no one knew about Jessaloup, or could possibly have found out! Stop panicking, Isabel! But I couldn't stop my heart from hammering a terrified drum roll in my chest. It sounded so loud in my ears that for a moment I couldn't hear anything else.

There was a fire exit at the far end of the room. I glanced back at the little group of scientists. Mr. Peake was leaning over Dr. Kreinstead's shoulder, squinting at what the geologist was pointing to. I turned and walked quickly to the door. I pushed on the horizontal metal bar, and the door swung open.

I found myself standing in an alley between two brick buildings.

Across the way, on the other side of a tall dumpster, Jessaloup was crouched below an open window.

"Jessaloup!" I hissed, dizzy with relief. He saw me, and gestured for me to be quiet. His eyes were wide with excitement.

Suddenly I heard it too.

A song. A Siren song.

twenty-five

IT was coming from the open window. I ran up to where Jessaloup was squatting. I was trying to be quiet, but accidentally stumbled over a crate filled with empty cans.

At the sound of the crash, the music stopped abruptly.

"Who's there?" someone inside called out.

"It's only us," I said. "Sorry."

I found myself staring into the blue eyes of a girl in her twenties, with a thick blond braid halfway down her back. "Hey, were you spying on me?" she said, looking from one to the other.

"No! Well, actually, we were just curious," I said, embarrassed. "The sound you were listening to... What *was* that?"

She smiled. "Did you like it? It's a whale song. The humpback whales sing, you know. *Megaptera novaeangliae.* I'm studying their song. Would you like to come in and listen?"

"Yes!" said Jessaloup before I had a chance to reply. "Yesss!"

The girl leaned out of the window and pointed to the end of the building. "Make a right at the end, there you'll see a door. Then walk back down the corridor; I'm in Room 104."

I had to run to catch up with Jessaloup. "Megaptera *what?*" he muttered.

"That's the scientific name for the Sirens," I explained. "It's Latin, I think. I don't remember what it means."

"It probably means *ugly humpback,*" Jessaloup snorted. (The singing ones call themselves the Sirens of the Sea; they consider it an insult to be called 'humpback', since they pride themselves on their sleek, streamlined bodies.)

"I bet it doesn't," I protested.

"Or something even worse," he said gloomily.

The girl with the blond braid was alone in Room 104, which was filled with racks of equipment and a large control board, like a music studio.

"What does Megaptera — uh, — mean?" I asked, hoping to prove Jessaloup wrong.

"Megaptera is the genus, the humpback whale," she said.

"*Told* you," Jessaloup muttered.

"*Megaptera* means 'great wing', for their powerful flippers."

At that, Jessaloup looked mollified. He smirked at me.

"And *novaeangliae* means from New England," she went on, "which is a pretty good description, since we see a lot of them right here off the coast of New England."

"I know," I said.

"You do?" she asked. 'So have you been on a whale watch?"

I nodded.

"Isn't that fun?" she said. "Did you see any whales?"

"Yes," I said. "I did."

Jessaloup turned his head away to hide a grin.

"So, what are you doing here?" she asked.

I quickly told her our names, and explained that we were visiting the institute with our science teacher. I tried to keep an eye on Jessaloup, who was pacing around the lab, peering behind the racks, looking for something.

"Where's your song box?" he asked abruptly.

"You mean the recording I was listening to?" she said. "Isn't that an intriguing sound? I'm studying the humpbacks' song. We are trying to work out what it could mean."

I sent Jessaloup a warning look not to say anything.

"Have you figured it out yet, then?" I asked innocently.

She smiled. "Well, no. Not at all." She sighed, "I wish we had. We've been trying for years, but to tell you the truth, we haven't got a clue. All we know is that it is definitely a song, not just random noises, since all the whales in any one part of the ocean normally sing the same pattern of sounds. We believe it's a form of communication. But it may also have something to do with mating, since it's the males, in general, that sing."

I felt myself blushing. I could feel Jessaloup's eyes on me.

"But actually," she said, "I think I may be on the verge of discovering something. Because something new is happening. Something quite unexpected."

"Really?" I asked. "What…"

"Really. I've just come back from an expedition at sea. Came in late last night. We were able to record hours and hours of whale song. But now that I've started playing it back, I'm noticing something unusual. The funny thing is — well, the tone and pattern seem to have changed quite radically. Just in the last week or so. In a different way than it ever has before."

"So?" I said breathlessly.

"So, usually the changes are more gradual; it can take months for the song to change in any perceptible way. Want to hear it?"

"Yess!" said Jessaloup. "Yess!" I sent him another warning look.

As she fiddled with a dial, she said, "My name's Alicia, by the way. I'm a marine biologist. I take it that you two are interested in marine life?"

"We are," I answered politely. "Uh — in whales, especially."

"Shhh," she said, flicking three switches up — click, click, click — but she needn't have said it, because, at the first notes of the song, Jessaloup and I both froze.

As I listened, spellbound, to the familiar bursts of sound, the chirps, the barks, the whoops and the booming roars, I found myself transported back to my home somewhere way out in the blue ocean, feeling the cool water sliding over my back as, with a flip of my strong tail, I slipped below the surface, where sound travels so very far and the song can be heard most clearly.

How I had missed hearing those thrilling calls!

Blinking away the tears that were making my eyes glaze over, I glanced at Jessaloup. His eyes were squeezed shut, his arms were rigid at his sides and his fists were balled. I could see that he was struggling with himself. I reached out and put my hand lightly on his arm.

There we stood, the warmth of his arm colliding with the warmth of my fingers, the two of us, I thought to myself, strangers in a dry land, yearning for home…

twenty-six

"So anyway, that's what it sounds like," Alicia said in a businesslike voice, switching off the recording. "The print-out shows a definite pattern, and it's quite unusual. A higher, more whiny pitch, the notes faster and more staccato."

"*Danger*," said Jessaloup in a low voice.

"Excuse me?"

"He means," I said quickly, "that he hears danger. He's — uh — very attuned to sounds, you know, he's — he's a musician himself, and..." I trailed off. I hoped Alicia wouldn't think we were making fun of her work.

"Danger? Well, I agree that it does sound urgent.

Almost like a call to arms. You may have something there," she said thoughtfully. "Although I don't know — I hadn't thought of it before, but maybe it *is* supposed to be some sort of warning…"

We both nodded eagerly. "That's it, that's what it sounded like," I said. "A warning."

"But of what?" said Alicia. "What could be so alarming?"

I stared at Jessaloup. If I told her what we knew, how to prove it? The only proof was Jessaloup and his funny-looking flipper-hand — but what if Alicia called the CIA, or Homeland Security, what if they declared that Jessaloup was an alien, and dragged him away for their scientific experiments, right here in this laboratory or some other secret location, what if they decided to dissect his flipper or something — I shuddered. I couldn't let that happen!

Just at that moment the door was flung open. "Here they are!" called Mr. Peake. "I've found them!" Two of Dr. Kreinstead's assistants followed him into the room.

"What have you two been up to?" Mr. Peake scolded us. "You're not supposed to go wandering off by yourselves! These two young men had to interrupt some very important work to help me find you!"

"Sorry, Mr. Peake," I said. "Jesse heard what sounded like a whale song, and we came in here to see what that was about." Turning to Alicia, I explained, "This is our teacher, Mr. Peake."

"Hey, Alicia, whassup?" said one of the young geologists, perching on the edge of her console. "Still worrying your pretty little head about those tuna tunes? Ha, ha, *tuna tunes* — get it?"

Alicia sniffed. "Get out of here, you moron. Just go back to playing with your rocks."

"Well alright then, chaps," he said in a put-on British accent. "I can tell when I'm not wanted. Glad we found the missing youngsters, Sir, but it's crunch time for us rock jocks. Back to REAL work. Toodeloo."

The two geologists thundered out of the room. Mr. Peake coughed awkwardly. Jessaloup and I looked down at our feet.

"Oh, don't worry, " said Alicia, laughing at our embarrassed faces. "That's my boyfriend, Trevor. It's the way we deal with each other around here. We don't really mean it. It's just scientific rivalry." She frowned. "Although I sometimes wish they'd all take me and my research more seriously. Crunch time, my foot!" She snorted, and turned back to her sound console.

"Actually," said Mr. Peake, "It's true. They weren't joking about that. I was just in there with them, and it seems that they've detected some unusual seismic activity in the North Atlantic." He gave Jessaloup and me a significant look. I clapped my hand to my mouth. He went on, "Their sensors are going crazy. They think it may be a volcano threatening to blow somewhere underneath the ocean. That's why they're so excited. And worried."

"Worried!" I couldn't help gasping. He nodded back at me grimly.

"Well, it isn't as if I'm not dealing with something very

unusual myself—" Alicia began. She stopped abruptly, and turned to Jessaloup. "Danger?" she said. "Didn't you say you heard danger, in the song?"

Jessaloup nodded.

Alicia stiffened, gathered up some papers, and said, "I've got to go talk to them."

We looked at each other. Mr. Peake raised his eyebrows at us. Then, without another word, we all ran after Alicia, who was dashing down the hall, out the door, across the driveway and into the building next door.

twenty-seven

BACK in the seismology lab, we found Alicia excitedly waving her papers at Trevor, who was gesturing at her to be quiet. They were obviously in the middle of a meeting; the room was full of people I hadn't seen before.

"No, listen to me a minute!" she was shouting. There were pink blotches on her cheeks and down the sides of her neck. She was all worked up. "You've all got to listen!"

"Pipe down!" Trevor hissed. "Do you really think we have time for that now?"

"What is it, Alicia?" asked Dr. Kreinstead, looking up from his monitors.

"I think there may be a connection between what I've been hearing and what you're observing…" she panted.

"How do you mean?" said Dr. Kreinstead, scratching his stubbly cheek.

"Sorry, Professor," said Trevor. "Alicia gets like this sometimes." Putting his hands on her shoulders to make her turn back toward the door, he said, "I'm sure it's very interesting, but can't you save it for another time…"

I couldn't help myself. "Will you SHUT UP a minute? *Listen* to her!" I yelled as loudly as I could, straining my voice so that it petered out in a coughing fit.

Jessaloup sent me an approving look.

All the geologists stared at me. I felt myself going red.

Dr. Kreinstead raised his eyebrows. "Well, let's hear it then, if it's so urgent," he said calmly.

Alicia took a deep breath. "Well, you know, I've detected an unusually abrupt change in the pattern of the whale song we just recorded," she said. "And I think it might very well have something to do with whatever is setting off your sensors…"

The geologists looked at her skeptically. Trevor was shrugging his shoulders apologetically, as if to say, Don't blame me.

"Alicia dear," said Dr. Kreinstead. "It's not that I don't respect your research on rorquals, but I really don't see the connection. No whale is large enough to set off a seismic event of *any* magnitude, you of all people should know that."

"No, that's not what I meant, of course not…" She looked around wildly. "Oh, shoot, I'll prove it to you!" she cried. "Just wait and see!"

I realized that Jessaloup, in his excitement, had slipped his arm around my back. Before I could acknowledge the gesture, Alicia had wheeled around and stormed out of the lab. The three of us trotted back after her.

We reached the biology lab just as Alicia was pulling a box of discs down off a shelf. She dropped to her knees and started digging through it. "Can we help you find something?" I asked.

She sat back on her haunches, and blinked, staring at us as if she'd forgotten we were there. "I'm trying to find the material some colleagues in Hawaii sent us," she finally said. "Recordings of humpback song in the Pacific Ocean around the time of the 2004 tsunami. I remember that they reported that there'd been an abrupt change in the Pacific Ocean song in the days leading up the disaster — so sudden that they wondered if it could have had anything to do with the event. They've reported a similar thing happening just before the devastating Japanese tsunami of 2011."

"As if the whales knew something was up," Mr. Peake said.

"Yes, but they haven't been able to prove it. Still, you know," Alicia went on excitedly, "there's been quite a lot of research recently on animals sensing danger — earthquakes, forest fires, tornadoes and such — before they happen. The question is how to harness that animal sensitivity, so that we could use it some day to predict natural disasters."

"What you're saying," I said slowly, "is, if you can

find those Hawaiian discs, and they show similar sound patterns to the ones you just recorded, you could—"

"Exactly," said Alicia. "Now where did I last see them? I know they're here somewhere." She stood up and started digging through the papers on the console where her laptop lay buried. "And I think I have some recordings from the South Pacific too, taken at the time of the Samoa quake of 2009, if I can find them."

"If they all follow the same pattern, you'll have your proof," Mr. Peake said.

"You got it," said Alicia grimly. "That's the breakthrough I need. Then it will mean something. Then those clowns will *have* to listen to me. Tuna? *I'll* show them who's a tuna!"

twenty-eight

Less than half an hour later we were climbing back into the minivan. Mr. Peake had already started the engine.

"What's the big hurry?" I panted. We'd had to run to catch up with him.

Once Alicia had found the older recordings and had started comparing the printout of their sound waves with her own more recent data, I had noticed Mr. Peake starting to get very fidgety, exhaling audibly through his nose and glancing at the door. Finally he'd looked at Jessaloup and me, raising his eyebrows and shrugging his head sideways meaningfully. "Well, if there's nothing more we can do to help, we ought to be going," he'd told Alicia abruptly.

"You've got this covered, I think. You don't need us getting in your way. Good luck."

"But…" I had started to protest, but Mr. Peake was already out the door. We'd had no choice but to follow him as he strode back to the parking lot without looking back.

So now, as I helped Jessaloup into his seatbelt — this time he'd climbed in next to me in the back seat — I demanded, "Why couldn't we have stayed a bit longer?"

"No need to wait around until they work it out," Mr. Peake said, frowning at us in the rearview mirror. "I do believe you kids put them on the right track. Well done, by the way. I'm sure that between Alicia's recordings and Kreinstead's instruments, they'll soon have enough evidence to sound the alarm. I give them a couple of hours, max, to come to the right conclusion. But we can't afford to waste any more time. If it's really happening this evening, I need to get back to pick up Mrs. Peake, and Bunsen." His voice cracked, and I could see sweat glinting on his upper lip and on the side of his face. "Sorry kids, but we've got to try and beat the rush — just think of the traffic once the evacuation order goes out! I don't want to get stuck in *that* traffic jam."

I have to admit that my jaw dropped. Here Jessaloup and I had been worrying about saving *everyone* — hundreds, thousands of people living along the coast and on the islands, and all Mr. Peake could think about was his own family! But as I stared at the back of his rigid neck, I softened a little. Mr. Peake was scared. He couldn't help it.

Which meant that he believed us, finally…

Mr. Peake read my mind. "I owe you an apology. I'm sorry I doubted you," he said. "Jesse, I hope you'll forgive me."

Jessaloup made no response. I looked over at him. He was sitting up very straight, staring out the window.

"Jessaloup," I said softly. I felt that maybe I hadn't been paying enough attention to him. I wondered what was going through his mind.

"Izzabel," he said flatly, almost mechanically. He kept his eyes on the landscape whizzing past.

"Are you mad at me?" I whispered.

"Mad?" he said. "Why?"

"I don't know — I just get this feeling you're, you know, disappointed in me or something."

Now he turned to look at me. His eyes were large and unblinking. He shook his head. "No."

"No? Not disappointed?"

"No." He swallowed. "Sick."

"You're feeling *sick*?" I said, alarmed. "What's the matter? Do you have a headache? Do you feel you're going to throw up?"

He shook his head. "No."

"Do you mean you're homesick? You miss the ocean?"

He cleared his throat. "No."

"Then *what?*" I said anxiously. He was looking so serious.

"You know. That song."

"Which song?'

"*Sick*."

"Oh," I said, my heart beating a little faster. I looked down, and saw his hand — the one wrapped in the Ace bandage, which, I noticed, was starting to get a little grubby — groping toward mine. I kept my hand very still — it seemed very important, for some reason, not to move, not even a fraction — and felt his hand hovering over mine.

Then our hands touched. It was only the lightest of touches, but it set off such an electric buzz, moving up my arm, my neck, then the back of my throat, that I had to swallow. *Gulp*. I hoped Jessaloup hadn't noticed.

But he kept his hand right where it was.

Trying to sound nonchalant and act normal, I started babbling, for Mr. Peake's benefit. I didn't want him looking back at us in the rearview mirror. "I suppose you're right, there's no time to waste. We've got to get back to warn everyone. Oh, and there's Gram, I have to make sure she's all right. My grandmother," I explained, "has trouble walking. And her two cats — I've got to help her round those up, they always hide when they sense something's up, they hate having to go in their carrier; and then there's my brother Jacob, I've got to warn him too, and make sure…"

And then I stopped talking, and we were both quiet for a long time, sitting side by side, our two hands — or rather, one hand and one flipper — just barely touching.

twenty-nine

WE had to stop for gas, and while Mr. Peake worked the pump, Jessaloup and I ran into the gas station mini-mart to buy some food. I was too excited to be hungry, but Jessaloup was another story. When we met back at the check-out counter, I saw six hot dogs, two giant sodas and three mega bags of chips in his basket. I made a mental note to lecture him about healthier choices, but this wasn't the time.

We began making plans. Mr. Peake said that he'd drop us off close to my house, so that we could get Gram and her cats ready, and that he'd stop by on his way out of town again to pick us up.

"But I have to find my brother," I told him, "so if we're not there, just go ahead."

Just as we were driving into Provincetown and saw the Pilgrim Tower looming up ahead of us, the radio, which was tuned to the local news station, started emitting short, shrill blasts.

"Shhh!" I shouted. "Here it is! Listen!"

"*This is a broadcast of the Emergency Alert System,*" we heard. "*This is not a test. Repeat, this is NOT a test. The national geological survey has issued a tsunami alert. A tsunami set off by an imminent earthquake in the Atlantic Ocean may strike the East Coast of the United States within the next six to twelve hours. An immediate evacuation order has been issued for the following areas: Cape Cod and the islands, Nantucket and Martha's Vineyard and all other low-lying areas. Please do not panic. Buses are being readied for those who do not have transportation. Follow the instructions of your local authority. Do not go to the beach. Stay away from the water. This is an urgent alert. Repeat, this is an urgent alert. This is NOT a test.*"

We saw people coming out of their houses, excitedly talking to their neighbors in the street. As we tumbled out of the van at the corner of my block, Mr. Peake warned again, "Remember, if I don't see you back here in half an hour, I'll assume you've made other arrangements!"

When we got to my house, I ran to the kitchen, with Jessaloup close on my heels. "Gram!" I yelled. "Where *are* you?"

We found her stretched out on the couch in the living

room. "I was just taking a little nap," she said, dazed. "What's the matter, Isabel?"

"Gram, get up," I panted, "You have to come with us. Take your pills and anything else you'll need in the next couple of days. We're being evacuated."

"Evacuated!" she exclaimed, wide-eyed. "My, my! Why?" She looked outside. "It's a perfectly lovely afternoon, I don't see any sign of a storm..."

"It's not a hurricane, it's an earthquake — a tsunami," I told him. "A big wave's coming."

"When?"

"Soon! We don't know exactly, but..."

"How do you know?"

"It was on the radio! Turn on the TV, I'm sure they're broadcasting the warning right now!"

Gram patted the sofa to find the remote. When she'd found it, she turned around and said,

"And who, may I ask, is this young man?"

"That's Jesse, my friend," I said quickly. "He's coming with us. Mr. Peake, my teacher, is picking us up."

Gram was staring at the TV, which was showing maps, charts and flashing warnings. "Oh, but what about my cats?" she quavered. "Buttons and Ginger, we'll have to find them, you'll have to find them for me, dear, and..."

"I know," I told her. "You just take care of packing your pills, and anything else you need, OK? But hurry. We'll take care of the cats."

As we raced up the stairs, Jessaloup, glancing around, said, "So this is your ... home?"

"Yes, my house," I said. I wished I could have given him a proper tour. I wanted him to like my house. But there wasn't enough time.

The cats weren't in Gram's bedroom, nor in my parents' or brothers' rooms. "Come," I said to Jessaloup, "let's look up in my room."

My room was on the third floor, in the turret. To be honest, I knew that if the cats weren't on the second floor, they probably weren't up there either. But I really wanted — *needed* — Jessaloup to see where I lived.

thirty

"My room," I said proudly, throwing open the door.

He stepped inside. At first he didn't say anything, gazing at the aquamarine walls, the blue rug and the sea glass on the windowsill, the seashells, starfish and arrangements of dried seaweed and coral. My friends often teased me about my room. They called it "The Aquarium." My brothers had another nickname for it: "Sea World." But I didn't care — it was mine, and I loved it. I picked up the largest, scruffiest stuffed animal from the bed and hugged it. "See, it's a whale," I said. "He's my favorite, I've had him since I was three. His name is Snorkel."

Jessaloup smiled. "Hey, Snorkel," he said. Then he looked up. "Ah," he said, pointing to the charts and marine life posters thumbtacked to the watery green ceiling.

"Yes," I sighed. "That's the last thing I look at every night, before I fall asleep."

We stared at each other for the longest moment. All I could see was his eyes — ocean-deep eyes — gazing into mine. I felt his eyes, my nose, his cheeks, my lips, drifting closer. The world trembled and held its breath.

"*Isabel!*" Gram called from downstairs. "Have you found them yet?"

We both stepped back at the same time. "Not yet, Gram!" I shouted, forcing my voice to sound normal. "They must be in the basement!"

We thundered back downstairs. The cats' favorite hiding place was in the wall behind the dryer, where it was usually impossible to get at them. But as soon as Jessaloup arrived at the bottom of the basement stairs, they came slinking out of the laundry room and started rubbing seductively against his legs.

As he bent to pet them, I said, "Keep them entertained. I'll go get their cage."

I returned with the cat carrier to find Jessaloup sitting on the steps with Buttons on top of his head and Ginger on his shoulder. They were purring darkly, and Jessaloup was purring right along with them. I couldn't help smiling. He was such an amazing mimic. Together we managed to coax both cats into the carrier.

Gram was astonished they hadn't put up any fuss. "They

must really like you," she told Jessaloup. "They usually scratch and bite like crazy, they just *hate* being locked up."

He stared at her. "They are *scared. They're* scared of the big wave," he said indignantly, as if that should explain it.

Gram looked startled, but before she could get any questions out, I took her arm and began walking her toward the front door. "Let's go, Gram," I said. "By the way, where's Jacob? We've got to make sure he's heard about this."

Gram put her hands to her mouth. "I don't know... Oh dear... No, of course! I do know. He told me he was going to the Battle of the Bands after school. He said not to expect him until..."

The Battle of the Bands! What was *wrong* with me? How could I forget! It was the most important event of the school year. And Tom's band was one of the four bands competing. All my friends would be there... What if the news hadn't spread yet? What if they hadn't heard... I had to go and warn everybody!

Just then the doorbell rang. Mr. Peake was standing on the doorstep. I could see Mrs. Peake and Bunsen sitting in the minivan.

"Here," I said, thrusting the cat carrier into my teacher's hands. "You take these, if you wouldn't mind, and my grandmother. OK? Jesse and I have to go find my brother. We'll catch a ride, don't worry. You go on ahead."

"But..." said Mr. Peake.

"Don't wait for us. We can always get on a bus," I said.

"All right, but don't dawdle," he cautioned, opening the

door for Gram. "The evacuation buses are assembling in front of Town Hall and outside the High School. They're getting ready to head out real soon."

"Don't worry!" I called over my shoulder. "See you later!"

thirty-one

THE Battle of the Bands was taking place on the school soccer field, in the shadow of the Pilgrim Tower. As we drew nearer, I realized that the news hadn't yet reached the crowd. From the earsplitting sound of it, the battle was already in full swing. There was no way the sirens could be heard over that racket. We felt the droning vibrations of bass and drums long before we could make out a tune. Jessaloup stopped to stare at the colorful balloons tied along the fence, bopping and snapping in the wind as if they were being used as punching bags by some invisible hand. "Come!" I yelled at him. "Over here!"

I knew a back way in, where you could squeeze through a gap in the fence and duck under the bleachers to snag a place up front. We emerged just a few feet from the stage that had been rigged up under the scoreboard. *FISHERMEN 00 · GUESTS 00*, it read helpfully in big blue letters.

"Izzy!" I heard someone screaming somewhere behind us. I turned, and there was Molly, waving her hands in the air. "Up here! We've saved you a seat!" I saw that she was with Kristen, Danny Cho and Ruth; Jacob was sitting two rows behind with his girlfriend Stephanie. I started gesturing wildly — *Get out, go, go!!* But they were grinning as they waved back, mouthing, *You're late!*

Idiots! They didn't get it!

The first band was just finishing its set — The Bumbadiers, a group from a rival school, Nauset High. Tom and his band mates were plugging in their instruments and checking their amps. My friends began stamping their feet and yelling, *Mariners! Mariners!*

I was trying to figure out the best way to climb onto the stage when Reggie Gribbs, the student council president, came bounding to the front and announced, "Let's hear it for our *own* champions, the Raging Mariners!" There was a deafening cheer, and Tom grabbed the mike with two fists.

"Are you READY?" he yelled.

"READY!" the audience roared.

I twisted my head down, trying to hide my face by hunching my shoulders, but it was too late. Tom had spotted me in the front row. He raised his eyebrows enthusiastically, as if to say, *What's kept you so long?*

"Wait," he called to his band mates, "Change of program, dudes. Let's start with that song I wrote. You know, *Beach Girl.*"

No, no, I started gesturing, crossing and uncrossing my arms in front of my chest to warn him not to start, *Don't! STOP!* But his hand had already come down on the guitar strings — *TWANGGG* — and his band mates fell in with an ear-shattering chord. For a moment I stood there, frozen, as the music rolled over us like a tidal wave.

> *I want her*
> *I need her*
> *Want to find her*
> *But where oh where...?*
> *Oh she's always out of reach,*
> *But you can find her on the beach,*

Tom pumped his fist in the air. There was a roar of approval as he swung his arm down, pointing straight at me.

She's mah BEACH GIRL...

Jessaloup, next to me, was not amused. His face was set; I saw the muscles in his cheeks clenching. I didn't know if it was the shouted lyrics, the squealing loudspeakers or Tom's gyrations, but he obviously didn't like the performance one bit. My classmates behind us, on the other hand, were really into it. They were screaming as if they were listening to the most awesome band in the world.

"I'm going up there," I shouted in Jessaloup's ear, and without waiting to see if he was following me, I hopped over the mess of electric cords on the ground and started climbing up onto the stage. Unfortunately Tom, beaming, thought I was coming up there to kiss him or something. I turned my cheek away just in time.

"Here she is! Let's hear it for Beach Girl!" Tom panted into the mike, grabbing my hand and raising it in the air like a prizefighter. Another loud cheer went up.

Pulling my hand away, I put my face up to the microphone.

"STOP!" I yelled as loud as I could. I felt my vocal cords nearly splitting from the strain. "STOP THE MUSIC I SAID!"

The band faltered on for a few more bars, then petered out.

"Oh come on, Isabel," hissed Tom. "Can't you take a joke? What is *wrong* with you?"

Pushing him away, I addressed the crowd. "I'm sorry, people, but you've all got to get out of here. There's no time to waste. There's a tsunami coming, the whole town is being evacuated…"

Tom tried pulling me away from the mike. "Are you out of your mind?" he hissed. "You're ruining our…"

Just then another round of alarm bells and sirens started up all around us. It began as a moaning sound but rapidly built up into a clashing, clanging, wailing, deafening screech. This time the crowd was able to hear it. I could see the expressions on the audience's faces change from goofy delirium to baffled horror.

"You see? There's the warning! This is not a joke," I yelled. "Everybody, get out of here!"

A policeman who had stepped onto the stage took the mike over from me. "Listen to the young lady here, please, folks, she's right. We are expecting a tsunami in the area. OK, OK, no need to panic! Now. We need each one of you to leave in an orderly fashion. Walk, everybody walk, don't run! There are buses outside to take you to higher ground. Don't try to find your cars, we want as few cars on the road as possible at this point, that way we can get you all out of here in time. There is room on the buses for everyone…"

The crowd was already swarming toward the exit. I saw my brother hopping down from the top bleachers, taking two benches at a time. "Jacob!" I yelled.

"Izzie!" he yelled back. "Get on the bus, OK?"

"I will! You too! No need to go home, Gram and the cats are already on their way, I took care of it," I shouted. He gave me the thumbs-up sign to show he had understood, and I turned to find Jessaloup.

Who, for a change, was nowhere in sight.

thirty-two

WHERE *the heck did he disappear to this time,* I fumed to myself. This wasn't funny. I knew that Jessaloup had a strong independent streak; I had admired him for that when he was in the ocean, but still, he was a stranger here, here he was supposed to listen to *me,* I knew my way around here and he did not, didn't he realize that this was no time to play games? The soccer field was emptying fast. Maybe he had been swept up in the crowd... I raced across grass that was getting trampled by hundreds of hurrying feet, and squeezed out through the gate.

I saw a familiar face ahead of me — Corinne, a girl in my class. I tapped her on the shoulder.

"Hey, Corinne, have you seen a tall kid — uh, well you know, who looked like he might be lost?" I asked, then immediately regretted it. Corinne did not get along with me and my friends. To be honest, we found her supremely annoying. But I was desperate.

She stared at me as if I was out of my mind. "You've got to be kidding," she squeaked in a panicked voice, her eyes rolling from side to side. "Why should I care? Oh my God — A tsunami, oh my God, I'm not a very strong swimmer, you know, who's going to save *me*? I'm going to *drown*!"

"No of course you're not, Corinne!" I snapped, brushing past her. "Just get on the bus, like everyone else!"

There were at least thirty buses parked outside the field – blue transit buses, white shuttle buses and yellow school buses. I squeezed past some kids climbing into the first one, and scanned the rows. No Jessaloup.

"Excuse me," I said, threading my way back through the pushing, shoving people desperate to get on, "sorry, coming through, pardon me."

I jumped down and tried looking inside some of the other buses by hopping up and down below the windows. The buses were rapidly filling up. The first ones were already roaring down the street.

"Get on the bus, Izz!" yelled my brother through the window of one of the buses as it started moving off.

"I will!" I shouted back at him. "Don't worry!"

A woman in a bathrobe and slippers standing near me began to scream. "I don't want to die!" she wailed. She was shaking so badly that I felt I had to stop and *do* something. But then a man — I guessed it was her husband — appeared from out of nowhere and took her by the arm. "Come on, Teresa, calm down," he shushed her, "I'm here, look, just come this way, you're going to be all right."

I looked around wildly. I couldn't leave without Jessaloup! I was responsible for him! What would happen to him if...

"There you are, Izzie!" said Kristen, out of breath, and "There she is!" panted Molly beside her. "We were looking for you. We wanted to make sure to get on the same bus as you. Come on!"

"I can't," I told them, "I need to find someone first."

"Who?" asked Kristen.

"Oh, a boy — You don't know him, he's a friend from camp, but he was just visiting me, I feel responsible for him..."

"What does he look like?" asked Molly. "You never told us about any friend from camp, hey! What's the big secret? What's he like?"

"He's tall, and, like, dark-skinned, with these dreadlocks, and he's wearing blue shorts and..."

"A Red Sox jersey? He *is*? Oh, we've seen him!" cried Kristen.

"*Where?*" I cried.

"Over there, near the school entrance, he's the one who got in a fight with Tom..."

A *fight*?

"What do you mean, with Tom?" I demanded. "What

do you mean, a fight?"

"Oh yeah, he gave Tom a bloody nose," said Molly, "but I don't think it's broken, don't worry. I've never seen Tom get so steamed. We don't know what it was about, but I heard it was your friend's fault, he started it by saying something insulting to Tom about his song, and then he kind of butted Tom with his head, and Tom caught him in a headlock, and…"

"Where is he now? Where did he go?" I croaked at my friends.

"Who, Tom? He's already on the bus," said Kristen. "Over there. The driver had a first aid kit and gave Tom an icepack. He's going to be all right. Anyway, we can't stand around here forever, we've got to *go*. Are you coming?"

"I — no, you go on ahead," I yelled at them over my shoulder. I ran over to the bus Kristen had pointed out. I could see Tom sitting inside, looking dazed. He was holding an icepack to his nose. I knocked on the window.

"Isabel! You!" he said, cranking open the window. "What the…"

"What happened?" I yelled at him. "What'd you say to him?"

"Your friend? The black kid? He almost broke my nose!"

"I'm sorry," I shouted, "but I've got to find him. I'm sorry about your nose, really! But what did you say to him, to make him so mad?"

"Me? Nothing! He came over to me, raving about how my song sucked, and then when I said he'd better watch himself with you, because you were my girl, he just went berserk!"

"Where did he go?" I sobbed.

"To hell, for all I care. Do you think I give a—...? Get on the bus, Isabel."

"No!" I yelled, starting to run. "Anyway, I'm not your 'girl,'" I shouted over my shoulder. "Not even your *Beach Girl*. Can't you get that through your stupid head?"

thirty-three

I RACED down the street, away from the departing buses and the dwindling crowd behind me. "*Idiot!*" I scolded myself as I ran through the town. What a dumb-ass I'd been! What must Jessaloup have thought when he'd heard Tom serenade me with a song he claimed to have written specially for me? Why hadn't I had the sense to put myself in Jessaloup's shoes, to see it from his — a whale's — perspective? I'd totally forgotten about Jessaloup's feelings! How could I have been so *stupid*?

In the Sirens' world, a song isn't just a *song*; it's something very profound. The Song contains your entire history. It's a mystery, it's an oracle, it's the traditions of your tribe and the wisdom of the world. It's a prayer and a devotion.

And when it's mating season, it's a declaration of love.

It wasn't until I had spent almost a year in the ocean and had grown very close to Jessaloup that I had finally come to understand that last part. When a male Siren chooses a mate, he must first prove his prowess by challenging or fending off any rivals. This can lead to some spectacular fights. If a whale wins his fight, he is allowed to go on to the next step and woo the female he loves. With a song. A song he composes and sings specially, and only, for her.

The whales had kept me in the dark about that little detail — until the day I'd accidentally witnessed a fight between two of my friends. When I had finally confronted my guardian, Onijonah, about it, indignant that this crucial information had been kept from me, especially in light of my feelings for Jessaloup, she'd explained that there could be no wooing for me. I was slated to return to the human world some day, which meant I wasn't supposed to form any lasting attachments and risk being claimed forever by the sea; I was too young, in human years anyway, she said, to make that decision for myself.

Even back then, I'd had enough sense to get it. What she meant was that if Jessaloup had been allowed to woo me, I could have ended up pregnant. And when that happens, you can never go back.

So, that's the story. Of course I *did* go back — back to my life on land. I thought I had to. And yet... I'd been agonizing over that decision ever since. That's what kept me up at night, that's what made me a bad friend and a sulky daughter, that's what made me feel so lost, sometimes. What if things had worked out differently for me? What if we hadn't been attacked by sharks, what if I hadn't been seriously injured, what if my wound had healed by itself, without the need of human medical intervention… What if I had stayed, after all?

I reached the fisherman's shack just as the sun was setting. I threw open the door. There was no sign of life in there. I ran down to the end of the jetty. The sea was empty except for the buoys bobbing up and down. I spread my arms hopelessly, and whirled around in a circle. Where else could he have gone? Was he deliberately hiding from me?

Next I tried our house, a ten-minute jog back into town. The streets were almost completely deserted by now. All the buses had left. At home I stormed up and down the stairs, looking into each empty room, calling *Jessaloup! Where are you?*

I was getting desperate.

The house was silent, stern, and maddeningly unresponsive.

I slammed the front door behind me. Where to go next? I started down the street. Suddenly I heard a police siren behind me. I jumped out of the way onto the sidewalk, but the police car drew up beside me, flashing lights and all.

"Where do you think you are going, young lady? Don't you know there's an evacuation order? Everyone has to leave."

"I know, officer, I'm meeting my parents, they're waiting for me just around the corner," I lied.

"Say, don't I know you?" the policeman said. "Aren't you the young lady who came into the station the other day?"

"Uh, maybe," I faltered. It was the officer who had made fun of me when I had gone there to speak to the Chief.

"So tell me, how did you know this tsunami was coming? Where'd you get the information?"

"Uh, I don't know — just a hunch, I guess."

"Just a hunch?" He was frowning. I thought, Great, now he's going to arrest me, but he went on, "Well, Miss, I must apologize for not taking you seriously. Normally we would investigate a report like that, but you have to understand that…"

"I understand," I said hastily. "But I have to go. They're waiting for me."

"Stay safe!" he called after me. "Get to higher ground — Now!"

I turned the corner. There, at the top of the hill looming ahead of me, the Pilgrim Tower solidly stood its ground, as if it, at least, had nothing in the world to worry about.

thirty-four

I DON'T know if you've ever been to the Pilgrim Monument in our town, but it's an important landmark, and we're proud of it, because this is where the pilgrims first landed when they came to America, before moving on to Plymouth Rock. It happens to be just up the street from our high school, and I would often go there after class and climb the sloping ramps and the 116 steps to the top (believe me, I've counted them). I'd go up there to stare through the openings in the thick granite walls, sometimes dropping a couple of quarters into one of the telescopes in hopes of catching sight of something on the horizon — the spray of a whale, maybe, or a shiny black back, or the flip of a tail, way out at sea. I was there so often that the museum staffers all knew me, and they usually let me in for free.

The gift shop was deserted. I ran out the back door and sprinted up the slope to the base of the tower; the gate was open, and I pushed my way inside

Clattering up the dark stairs and storming up the ramps, I reached the top of the tower in about five minutes — a record. As I bolted up the last set of stairs, I realized that it was already pitch black out, too dark now to see anything from up there. My lungs bursting, I leaned against the granite wall to regain my balance. I was feeling a bit dizzy. Was it because I'd run up here so fast? My head was spinning. I sat down with my back against the wall. I would wait here, I decided. Higher ground, the policeman had said. You couldn't get any higher than this! And maybe Jessaloup would come to the same conclusion, and find me up here…

I must have fallen asleep, because the next thing I knew, someone was roughly shaking me awake. I opened my eyes. But there was no one there.

Was I hallucinating? Ouch! The back of my head was banging against the stone floor. What was happening to me? Everything was jumping around like crazy, I couldn't get my eyes to focus…

It wasn't me, I realized as I tried getting to my feet — the floor itself was shaking! The whole tower was shaking…

EARTHQUAKE!

I clawed at the wall closest to me, but my hands couldn't seem to get a grip anywhere. I felt one foot slide in one direction, the other in the opposite direction. My teeth were chattering in my mouth, and my molars snapped down hard on the inside of my cheek. Yee-ouch! My spine was rattling as if the vertebrae were about to come loose and shake my head right off my neck. Was I coming apart? Would the tower hold, or was it, too, about to break apart, stone by stone, and spit my body out into the void piece by piece?

When the shaking finally stopped, I was curled into a little ball on the cold stone floor, my nose tucked between my knees like a terrified mollusk. Dazed, I dusted myself off and staggered to my feet.

I was still all in one piece. The tower too was still standing, although I saw that the big telescope at the southwest corner of the observation deck had toppled over.

I peered out the window closest to me. How long had I been asleep? The moon was out now, a brilliant full moon, bathing the town in a ghostly grey light. Everything down below looked pretty normal — except that there were no people.

The people were gone.

And then I saw that the flagpole on Fisherman's Wharf was on the ground, and the dilapidated shed next to the hardware store had collapsed, and some of the cars in the parking lot had rolled into a giant heap.

I shook my head, to clear it. I was still shaking inside. Concentrate, Isabel! You came up here because… What was I doing here? Why had I come up here again?

Because there was going to be a tsunami — And we had managed to sound the alarm, and got the whole town evacuated just in time, Jessaloup and I, we had done it…

Jessaloup!

I had climbed up here to see if I could spot Jessaloup!

Jessaloup, who had been in a fight, and who must have thought, just because I'd been so distracted, and just because another boy had sung to me, that he had lost his claim on me — because he didn't understand! He didn't understand *anything!*

It was my fault. I should have taken the time to explain things to him. I shouldn't have assumed that he would know that in the human world, being in love didn't depend on winning a fight, or hearing a song.

I ran to another window, this one facing away from the harbor, toward the airport. There was no sign of life down there. I climbed over the fallen telescope and leaned out of a third window.

And there, in the direction of the sand dunes, I saw a moonlit figure, all alone except for his own long black shadow undulating over the ground at his side. He was walking away from the town.

It was him. I could tell even from this distance, from the way he walked, powerfully, leaning forward, swinging his arms as if he were plowing through the waves.

"Jessaloup!" I yelled, waving my arms.

I tried again, screaming as loud as I could.

But the wind muffled my voice and swallowed it up. I could barely even hear myself screaming, as if my ears were plugged with cotton wool.

Jessaloup did not turn around.

thirty-five

GETTING down took even less time than going up. I practically tumbled down the stairs, bumping my elbow into the sidewall at every turn, slithering down the ramps. On one of the upper landings I almost ran into three elderly people sitting on the floor. I stared at them, and they stared back at me, backing up against the wall to let me through.

"Oh, don't go out there, dear!" said one of the ladies. "There's a big wave coming, you know. You'll be safer in here."

"Just in case," said the old man, "Better safe than sorry. Though I still can't believe it, a tsunami, here, in our lifetime! Who ever heard of such a thing? We don't want to be evacuated, I told them. We'll be fine in our house."

"Stubborn old coot, you are, Dad! But aren't you glad you decided to listen to me in the end?" said the second woman.

"When Judy came looking for us," quavered the old lady, "and we realized we had missed the last bus, she made us come up here. It's our best chance of saving ourselves in case of a flood. It's the highest spot for miles."

I nodded as politely as I could as I squeezed past them. I didn't have the time for a conversation. I hoped they would understand.

"*In case?*" the daughter groaned. "Didn't you feel the ground shaking just now? Honestly! What do you think that was? That was an earthquake, dear. It's for real!"

"What's that young girl doing?" I heard behind me; I was already two flights below them. "Doesn't she know it's not safe down there? Stop her!"

"Stop!" commanded the old man, yelling down at me, his voice echoing in the hollow space. "Come back, young lady!"

I flew downstairs, out the door and down the hill as fast as I could go, my feet slapping on the deserted pavement, straight down the middle of the silent streets, in the direction of the dune shacks, which was where I had last seen Jessaloup walking, headed for the beach.

At the foot of the dunes, I kicked off my sandals and started bolting up the path, flicking up cold, sticky sand at my legs as I ran.

When I reached the ridge, I gasped.

thirty-six

IT was an awesome, eerie sight.

Where I'd expected to see a narrow strip of beach between the dunes and the sea, there was now nothing but sand. Nothing but drying sand, rocks and shells glinting in the moonlight. No waves. No water to speak of. A vast sloping beach, stretching as far as the eye could see.

As I started down the slope, I found myself having to thread my way between little pools teeming with helplessly flopping fish. Thousands of stranded silvery fish gasping for water. I didn't want to think about what it meant. I plodded forward, my feet heavy in the soft, sucking sand. My mind strangely blank, I urged myself on, on, toward that coldly glistening horizon.

But then, suddenly, a picture popped up in my brain — an unwelcome thought. It was something I'd seen on TV about the great Indian Ocean tsunami. The tsunami that had struck Thailand and Indonesia without warning one terrible winter. You saw curious onlookers who had gathered excitedly on the beach to watch the sea retreating, exposing the ocean floor for an unprecedented distance. They'd started collecting shells. They hadn't realized what it meant. A huge wave was about to come crashing in, and sweep them up in its deadly surge.

Three thoughts flashed through my brain.

One: Where's Jessaloup?

Two: What am I *doing*?

Three: I'm so stupid. I'm going to die.

And then I saw him. A bold, self-confident figure in the distance, arms swinging loosely at his side. He was strolling away from me, down toward the invisible sea. Too far away to hear me.

Look around, Jessaloup! I begged him wordlessly. *Come back…*

A great gust of wind lifted my hair off the nape of my neck and whipped it around my face. I spread my arms to steady myself.

Then, suddenly, out of nowhere, there it was. A wall of grey rising on the horizon. A horror-movie nightmare, or an extreme-surfer's dream — water, dangerous water, swelling, flinging up spume, thundering toward Jessaloup at an easy speed.

I stared helplessly as the wave advanced, rose, blotting out the stars. Now it was towering above Jessaloup, and…

Jessaloup calmly swung his arms back. The whole ghost-scene unfolded as if in slow-motion: just as the wave was about to topple over on top of him, he stretched his arms over his head, like a platform diver at the Olympics, took a great, taut leap into the air — and dove elegantly into the glassy wall head-on.

Stunned, for a fraction of a second I stood there paralyzed.

Then I turned and began to run, stumbling, back toward the dunes. But I could already taste the prickly salt on my tongue, and before I had taken more than three paces I felt myself being swept up off my feet and sucked backwards. A huge weight crashed down on me and tossed me around topsy-turvy in the swirling water like a helpless piece of driftwood.

I gasped, and tried to claw my way to the surface to take a breath, but the water closed over my head before I could pinch my lips shut. Water gushed into my nose, mouth and throat.

One last thought flashed through my mind:

This is the end.

Then everything went black.

thirty-seven

In my dream I was floating on top of the sea. I felt prickly salt drying on the flanks of my nose. I didn't feel like opening my eyes, because it felt so good, lying there like a princess, being rocked gently up and down. The fear was gone, the fear of minutes — or was it seconds, or maybe hours? — ago, when I'd found myself in my worst nightmare ever, running, stumbling over the exposed ocean floor, trying to get out of the path of that colossal wall of water bearing down on me...

Was I dreaming, or was I well and truly dead?

I sat up abruptly, and banged my head on something.

Ouww!

Rubbing my head, I opened me eyes. Where was I?

I was lying on something lumpy, but not altogether uncomfortable — a bed of some sort. A fringed canopy hung down above me — that was what I'd bumped into just now. It looked like a raggedy set of vertical blinds.

Rolling over, I gazed out through a gap in the blinds at a pale moon streaked with thin wisps of dark cloud. My bed moved under me, and some water came gushing in over the slick black sides that looked like giant inner tubes. Was I in some kind of inflatable raft?

Draping my arms over the side, I pulled myself up a bit, and looked out. Tiers of white-capped waves stretched to the horizon, like the frosting on a humongous layer cake.

My bed heaved, I heard a loud *Whoosh*, and then my view was obscured by a heavy, salty mist raining down.

What was *that*? Was it…?

Yes it was.

The noise a whale makes when it spouts.

Dazed, I drew my head back in, and rested there for a moment, to think. What had happened? Was I a whale again? I raised my hand to my eyes, just in case…

But it was a human hand. My own ordinary, disappointing, five-fingered hand. I gazed up at the swaying canopy above me…

Suddenly I knew where I was. It wasn't a bed canopy. It was a set of baleen plates. I was riding inside a whale's mouth.

No! Could it be — was it possible…?

I took a deep breath. "Uh — hello?" I called.

"Izzabel. You're awake."

Jessaloup's voice. Jessaloup's so very familiar, so very dear, so very welcome Siren-voice, coming from deep inside his whale's belly.

"Is that *you*?" I asked, my voice shaking with hope.

"Yeah."

"Can you understand what I'm saying?"

"I understand," came the rumbling answer. "Why shouldn't I understand?"

"It's just that I still seem to be, um, human, and you…"

"And I'm whale again. So? What difference does it make?" He sounded a little defensive. A little aggressive even, I thought.

"What happened?" I asked. I was still wondering if it was a dream.

"The big wave took you. I saw it happen, and grabbed you."

I collapsed backwards, weak with gratitude.

"You saved my life! Jessaloup, you saved my life! You rescued me from the tsunami!" I couldn't get over it. It seemed the most romantic thing in the world — to be snatched from the jaws of death by Jessaloup's giant jaws.

He blew a loud snort. *"Genius!"* he rumbled.

"Genius? Yes, you are, Jessaloup," I said gratefully, patting the skin of his gums.

"No, I meant *you* — the opposite, you know. You should have gone with your *friends*."

"Oh, I see." I had forgotten that I'd used the "genius" example when I'd tried to explain human slang to him. "You mean that I'm an *idiot*."

"Well, do you call that smart, following me down to the sea like that? You should have saved yourself."

I sat up, and bumped my head on the baleen again. It was all coming back to me.

"But I couldn't just let you go like that — thinking..."

"Thinking what, beach girl?"

Beach girl?? I could have strangled him right then, if he'd had a neck or anything small enough to fit my hands around.

I took a deep breath. "Jessaloup... You just don't get it, do you."

"Oh, I get it. I got it!"

"No you don't, because I don't give a hoot about Tom. I don't even really *like* him."

"He sang to you," he grumbled. "I heard it myself."

"But it's different! It's not the same, in the human world! To humans a song is just a song, it isn't important at all! Just because someone decides to sing someone a song, doesn't mean that they're going to hook up..."

Jessaloup didn't say anything. I noticed that he was being careful to stay at the surface, to keep me from getting drenched. So — he couldn't be *that* mad at me, could he? I cast around for the right thing to say.

"Humans who sing songs don't do it because they're, like, in *love*," I said. I blushed. "I mean, sometimes they do, but most of the time it's just for fun."

Still he didn't say anything. But I thought I heard a low, rumbling moan.

"You know what that word means, don't you?" I insisted.

"Love?"

"Sick," he said. Then he coughed, as if embarrassed. As if he wished he hadn't said it.

"That's not it…" I began. Then I said, "Oh, I remember. *Love Sick*. The song on my iPod! That's it, isn't it? I get it now."

"Hmpf," he said.

There was a long silence between us. My head was in a whirl.

"So, anyway. It's *you* I'm — uh — sick about," I finally blurted out. I couldn't believe I'd said it. "You, Jessaloup."

"Urgh," he rattled. "Really? *Me?*"

"Really," I said. "You."

For a moment I didn't know what was happening — the walls around me were tightening. I braced myself.

"Hang on there!" I heard him warn.

I felt myself being pushed up against the baleen plates as his jaw clamped shut. "Hold on tight!" he shouted.

I felt Jessaloup spin around. I knew that maneuver! He was getting ready to breach — he was diving down, down… gathering speed to leap straight up out of the waves. I clung on for dear life. My stomach lurched and plummeted — the way it feels when you're in a super-fast elevator.

We landed on the surface with an almighty crash, a whale of a belly-flop.

I just lay there for a moment, stunned. Then, when I thought it was safe to let go to wipe my face and shake the water out of my hair, I sputtered, "OK, what was *that* for?"

"Joy," was the answer.

thirty-eight

THE sea was calm. We were lapped in deep blue stillness. We were by ourselves; all the other sea creatures, whether asleep or not, had apparently decided to leave us alone.

I had lowered myself off the edge of Jessaloup's jaw, paddled around and found a safe position near his midsection. I now lay stretched out on my stomach on top of his right flipper at the shoulder joint, where, if I pulled myself forward a bit, I could gaze directly into his right eye.

"This is so weird," I said, "being together like this." We were moving slowly forward through the water, and I was enjoying trying to match the rhythm of my own breathing to his — four breaths to every blow. "I wish I'd turned back into a whale again, though. Like you."

"That would have made things easier," he agreed.

"I wonder why I haven't?" I said. "Can you change only once, then, from human to whale and back again, or in your case the other way round? — Do you know?"

"I don't know," he said slowly. "Don't you remember what Indigoneah told you, when you said goodbye the last time?"

"What did she say?" I asked, although I actually remembered it well. It had become a mantra in my head.

"Anything is possible. That's what she said."

"In other words," I said dreamily, "nothing's impossible."

We just drifted for a while, enjoying the vast hush of the night. Suddenly Jessaloup made a sideways swipe with his flipper. "What was *that* for?" I asked sleepily.

"Jellyfish," he growled. "Whole swarm of them. Wouldn't want the nasty little critters to sting you."

"Thanks," I said.

"Aren't you getting cold?" he asked.

"No, I'm warm enough for now," I said. His body heat was keeping the front of my body warm; if my back and shoulders got cold, I could turn around and lie on my back for a while.

I had started telling him all the things I hadn't told him before. I'd been too worried, too excited, too busy, or maybe just too embarrassed to talk about such things. How much I had missed him and the rest of my whale family, for instance; how long it had taken me to get used to my landlubber life again; how I had felt like a fish out of water. Now that Jessaloup was a whale again, the stuttering awkwardness between us was gone. We seemed to have resumed our old, familiar roles — that of two best friends, happiest in each other's company, bursting to tell each other everything. And there was so much to tell! Three years of being apart. Three long, lost years.

I wanted to know all about my whale family. Jessaloup reported that Onijonah was expecting another calf. "How about Mistenbel, is she big now?" I asked. Mistenbel had been just a couple of months old when I'd last seen her.

"She's at least as big as you were then," he said, teasing. "A big strapping thing. She's very mischievous, and gets into all sorts of trouble."

"What sort of trouble?"

"Oh, the other day, she decided to go off on her own and follow a gang of porpoises who lured her into the shallows. She nearly got herself stranded on the reef! It's lucky she isn't full grown yet, or she'd have come away with some nasty cuts and scrapes, I tell you."

He told me that our buddy Lemmertail, who had never yet won a fight, had left the pod and was living as a solitary, though they did sometimes bump into him on the big migration. The other mothers, Dilgruel and Feeonah, had each had another calf. Delight and Tomturan, their yearlings, were growing by leaps and bounds. "You should see Tomturan, he eats everything in sight, I've never seen a whale as hungry as he is. I bet he's going to be at least as big as Momboduno."

I was happy to hear that there had been no further mishaps with propellers, nets or fishing lines for our pod. But Jessaloup had heard that an entangled Siren in a distant sea had been rescued. Wielding sharp shells, the other whales had managed to saw through the cords. "The way you showed us, Isabel, when Dilgruel was caught in that net, that time."

"But — how did they know how to do it?" I asked. "Who showed them?"

"All the whales know by now. It's all over the ocean. How to cut through a rope with a shell. It's in the Song," he said. "You're a hero, you know. In the Song."

I was glad he couldn't see me blush. I thought of my Kids-for-Whales club. All those petitions — but none of them could ever come close to what I had managed to achieve when I'd been a whale, just by trading some elementary, common-sense human knowledge with the whales.

"Will you sing it for me?" I asked shyly. "I mean, the part about me, about freeing Dilgruel from the net?"

"All right," he said. "I can sing you that part."

I nestled my glowing cheek against his side as he took a couple of deep breaths and started singing. I closed my eyes, to let the sound penetrate deep inside my head.

When Dilgruel was caught in the net we nigh on gave up hope
But Izzabel the mermaid sawed through that rope
She was not afraid. The Sirens held their breath
But for that clamshell it would have been Death

for our dear sister Dilgruel as it was for Deepanorah
of the shapely tail twelve summers afore her …

"Deepanorah?" I interrupted him. I remembered hearing that name before. "Who was that?"

"Oh," said Jessaloup, "another Siren. She was strangled in a net. She died. Long time ago."

"Oh yeah?" I said. "I do remember hearing about her."

"She was missed," said Jessaloup. "She still is."

"But what was so special about her? Was she beautiful?" I remembered hearing my own flukes compared to Deepanorah's, so I was curious.

"She was," replied Jessaloup. "Although I was very young when she died, so I don't remember her that well myself." He paused a moment, then went on, "I think it's because her death was so tragic that everyone still talks about her."

I waited for him to say something else, like that I was beautiful too.

He hummed, but didn't say anything.

"So, anyway. What about you?" I finally asked. "What have you been up to since I left?"

'Oh, not much," he said, "Hanging around with the gang. Feeding ourselves silly up north in the summer, and then living the life down south in the winter. Scaring off sea lions. Ringing. Pinging."

"And…" I said carefully, "singing, of course."

"Yes," he said modestly, "some good singing. Much better than your friend Tom. His song really sucked, you know."

I laughed. "I am *so* over Tom and his stupid song. OK?"

"OK," he snorted, with an indignant whoosh.

I was quiet for a minute or so. Then I couldn't help asking, "So — who have you sung to? You know, your special Song?"

He coughed, swinging his flukes, which set up such a backwash that it almost swept me away; I had to cling on to his flipper for dear life.

"Was it Blossamer?" I sputtered, spitting out a mouthful of seawater.

"Blossamer?" He laughed. "No way!"

I suddenly had a lump in my throat and a piercing jab of sadness deep down inside. I didn't feel like asking any more questions. I didn't want to hear that he'd picked someone like that stuck-up Olgineah, who thought all the males were after her, or Falandrex, who'd once confessed to having a crush on Jessaloup. I didn't want to hear any more about beautiful females, whether dead or alive.

I looked up at the sky, which was rippling with stars, as vast as the ocean. I was going to tell Jessaloup about that, about how all those stars seemed to be a reflection of the sea, rather than the other way around, but all that rippling, all that twinkling, all that shimmering around me, up and down and sideways, was making my eyes tired. I would just close my eyelids for a second, and then I would…

thirty-nine

I woke up to find myself stretched out on Jessaloup's back under a hot, sizzling sun. "Hey, how long have I been asleep?" I croaked, rubbing my eyes. "I didn't mean to…"

"It's OK," he said. "You were very tired."

I licked my lips, which were swollen and parched. "I'm hot," I complained. "I've got to take a dip."

I slipped off his back and swam a few yards beside him. But my limbs felt heavy and stiff, my head too light, my eyes stinging and burning, and I soon climbed back on board his flipper. It was a relief to just lie there for a while.

I was terribly thirsty. "What do you have to drink around here?" I joked.

He started to say something, but I interrupted him. "Never mind, don't worry."

I rested my head on his shoulder, and trailed my hand in the water — the seawater that looked so inviting, so refreshing, but that would not quench my thirst. Whales, of course, don't need fresh water to drink — they get it from their food, or their blubber. It was *so* not fair, I thought to myself vaguely.

"Lucky you," I murmured.

"Lucky?" he asked.

"And lucky me," I added hastily. "Being with you. Here in the ocean." I tried to make it sound convincing. Because I did feel safe here, with Jessaloup. Although I didn't love feeling the way I was feeling right then, a bit light-headed and sick to my stomach.

To make myself think of something else, I considered the size difference between us: how small I was, how big he was in comparison. His flipper alone was three times as long as I was tall. It was amazing! But what did it matter — big or small, we were together, that was what mattered.

I just wanted it to go on like this — the two of us drifting on top of a watery world — forever.

The next time I tried opening my puffy eyes, the sun looked like a squished orange football on the horizon slowly melting into the sea. "Dinner time already!" I joked weakly. I realized that the nagging, upside-down feeling in my stomach was hunger. But I wasn't about to tell

Jessaloup; if he could go for months on nothing but his own blubber, then I should be able to hold out for a bit longer without complaining.

Jessaloup rolled carefully onto his side, stretching his flipper up in the air. I found myself sliding into the water. "Hey — watch what you're doing," I protested, grabbing hold of one of the folds of his throat just in time.

"Get in," he said, opening his jaw. "Come on, you can ride sitting in front of my baleen. That way you don't have to hold on all the time. And you've been getting too much sun out there. You're turning red."

I did as he said; for it was true, my arms were getting awfully tired, my skin was on fire, and it was a relief to sit cross-legged just inside his mouth, looking out. Just as I was settled in comfortably, we began to pick up speed.

"Where are we going?" I asked froggily. "What's the hurry?"

He didn't answer. Maybe he didn't hear me, because he was making a lot of noise, snorting and blowing through the waves.

I took in deep gulps of the sea air, feeling the stiff breeze flattening my cheeks, getting splashed in the face with bucketfuls of salt water every so often, and it was as if I was standing on the prow of my very own ship, steaming toward the edge of the world, where the sky and the sea and the land all converged and blended together into a bright new kingdom — fish, birds, animals, whales and humans all getting along as equals.

forty

"Izzabel. Wake up!"

I lifted my pounding head, shivering, and looked out.

I was staring at the hull of a ship, not a hundred yards in front of us.

I shook my head, to try to clear it. A thousand sticky cobwebs were lodged between my ears. My tongue felt swollen to twice its normal size, and when I opened my mouth to speak, my lips stuck together as if a bubble of bubblegum had popped all over my face.

"Wherrrarrh we?" I managed.

"I am dropping you off here," I heard him say. His voice sounded almost as thick and reluctant as mine.

"Drop me off! What do you mean!" I protested.

"See that boat? It's a rescue boat," Jessaloup said. "Get on my back. Then you'll have to wave, and shout at them."

"But I don't want to be rescued!" I cried. "Jessaloup, please! What are you doing! I want to stay in the ocean, with you!"

"You can't," he said simply. "I can't let you die."

"I'm not going to die!" I blubbered. "As long as we're together, I'll…"

"Humans can't survive in the ocean," he said. "You need fresh water to drink. And it's too cold for you in here. What did you call it, hypo, hypo…"

"Hypothermia," I muttered.

"Yeah. If you stay, you'll die."

"Not true!" I protested.

"You told me so yourself, back on land, remember? You wouldn't let me spend even one night in the sea."

"But that was different!"

"You have already been in the sea much too long. Your skin is starting to blister, and now you're turning blue. You've got to get out."

"No!" I wailed. "I can't go back! I don't feel cold! I have to stay with you! Please, Jessaloup! I'd rather die! If I die, I die! It's my choice!"

I saw the ship getting closer. Jessaloup was heading straight for it.

"Please," I begged. "I *know* that I'm meant to be in the ocean! I was never meant to live on land! Ask Onijonah, ask Momboduno, ask Indigoneah, ask anybody! They'll tell you…"

Jessaloup groaned. "Do you think I wanted this to happen?" He sounded angry now. "But I can't let you die like this. I have to save you."

"Did you hear that?" I heard someone shouting high above us. "That sounded like a whale's blow, didn't it? What the heck?"

"I don't understand," I yammered softly. "I thought you…"

"Stop it, Isabel," Jessaloup rumbled under his breath, "I'm not listening."

He let out another deliberate *whoosh*, which was immediately followed by another shout from the sailor. "It's definitely a whale. Come see!"

"Isabel! Shout for help! Now!"

"No way," I rasped. But he had already pushed me into the water, and immediately ducked underneath me.

"Wave your arms!" he hissed. "So they can see you!"

"I won't!" I spluttered, flailing around in the water, trying to find where he was in the dark. "Come *BACK*!"

"Didn't you hear something?" I heard the sailor call. There was a clatter of footsteps on deck. "That wasn't a whale. I heard a voice!"

Someone else was yelling, "Captain, cut the engine, I think we have a survivor!"

A bright searchlight came on, and swept over us. Or over me, for Jessaloup had sunk below the surface. I could feel him hovering a couple of feet below me. I made a feeble attempt to dive down after him, but it was too late.

I had been spotted.

Five minutes later I was lying on the ship's deck, weeping and coughing and flopping around like the prize catch of the day.

forty-one

THERE were just three people unaccounted for and presumed dead in the tsunami. With my "rescue" at sea two days later, that number went down to two. Everyone said it was a miracle that not more lives had been lost in the East Coast disaster. The advance warning and the authorities' quick response had led to a flawless evacuation all up and down the seaboard. There was a ton of damage, of course. Some houses along the shore had been swept away, some roads made impassible, boats and cars smashed, livestock drowned. But our town had largely been spared, protected by the dunes hemming it in on three sides. Our house was still standing, although the basement and first floor had quite a bit of flood damage and had to be repaired and repainted.

I was airlifted to a hospital in Boston. I don't remember much of my rescue, but I'm told that I fought those Coast Guard sailors tooth and nail. They say I tried to jump overboard, and in the end they'd had to tie me down on a stretcher to restrain me. I do remember the *wop-wop-wop* noise of the helicopter, which made me think I had somehow landed in a war zone. There was a nurse on board who kept trying to shush me, telling me that everything would be all right, that I was going to be all right.

Everything was not going to be all right. I knew that much as soon as I woke up in that pale green hospital room, hooked up to all kinds of IV bags and machines, with a tube up my nose and my family anxiously hovering around the bed.

"She's awake!" cried my mother. Leaning over me so that I could feel her soft breath on my face as she spoke, she said, "Don't try to talk, sweetie. Just rest. I'm here, don't worry, I'm not going anywhere. You've had an accident, and you've been very sick. But everything's going to be all right."

My head was pounding. I tried to sit up, but they wouldn't let me. Or maybe I just didn't have the strength. I started twisting my head from side to side on the pillow. "No, no, no, no!" I moaned. I meant that I didn't want to be all right, I didn't want to be in any hospital room, on dry land.

I wanted to be back in the sea.

forty-two

THEY say I drifted in and out of consciousness for three weeks. All I remember is that every time I opened my eyes I'd find myself lying on that same bed, staring at pale green walls, with the heavy linen sheet pressing my body down into the mattress and the monitor beeping and the I.V. drippity-drip-dripping. Sometimes I'd see one of my parents or brothers sitting in a chair next to the bed, and I'd feel so desperately helpless and weak all over that I'd give up and close my eyes again.

When I was finally able to sit up in bed, my back ached, my neck was stiff, and my dry tongue was stuck to the parched roof of my mouth. As soon as I realized where I was, I started crying. The dry air, the bedclothes, the scratchy hospital gown, all chafed at my skin. I couldn't seem to stop crying. At least the wetness and salty taste of my tears (so like the taste of the ocean) was some consolation.

I was an "interesting medical case," apparently, since every doctor and medical student in the hospital had to come to have a look at me. After a few of these visits, I realized it was the way my skin looked that interested them the most. Once the blistery sunburn started peeling off, the skin underneath had this pale, grayish cast to it, as if the sea had drained all the color from me. The doctors hummed and rubbed my arms with their thumbs and cleared their throats and ran all sorts of tests on me, but they wouldn't tell me what they'd found.

My parents brought me tempting things to eat and get-well cards from everyone I knew. Jacob and Alex (my oldest brother was home for the summer) tried to cheer me up with silly jokes and YouTube videos. Gram smuggled one of her cats, Buttons, into the hospital inside her big handbag, to show me that everyone in our family was accounted for. Molly and Kristen showed me pictures on their phones of the devastation, and shared stories of how the rest of our gang had fared in the disaster. They pretended not to notice my funny looking skin, or the tears that kept welling up, no matter how hard I tried to smile.

"Tom sends his best," Kristen reported. "He says he's not mad at you any more."

"Mad at me? What for?" I said listlessly.

"You know — your friend, that boy Jesse, almost broke

his nose when we were getting on the buses. Don't you remember? Tom said he wasn't going to visit you in the hospital because he wasn't sure if you'd want to see him."

"He's right," I said. "I'd rather not see him just now."

"Is that what you're so depressed about?" asked Molly. "Because, I mean…"

"No," I said. "I'm not at all sad about Tom. That isn't it."

"What happened to the other kid, anyway?" asked Kristen. "That black boy. Did he go home?"

"Yes. He's home again," I said, turning my head away so that they wouldn't stare. The tears were back again.

"Well," said Kristen awkwardly, getting up from her perch on the side of the bed, "we'd better get going."

My parents came in just as Molly and Kristen were leaving. They whispered something to them in the doorway. "We will," promised the girls, and I heard them skipping down the corridor. With a pang, I thought to myself that I didn't think I'd ever skip like that again, happy and carefree.

My mother was shaking her head. "See? She's not getting any better," she said to Dad.

Dad sat down on the edge of my bed. "All those tears!" he said. "Is it so bad?"

I nodded, and blew my nose.

"Where exactly does it hurt?"

Wordlessly, I pointed to my chest.

"Her heart," Mom told Dad. "She means, her heart aches."

I nodded again, although I didn't think they could possibly understand.

forty-three

A COUPLE of days later, I had a visit from Mr. Peake. He brought me a cheesecake that Mrs. Peake had baked for me. The sight of it made me gag, but I said politely, "Oh, that's so sweet of her, please tell her thanks!"

"And look who else I've brought to see you," Mr. Peake said, waving at someone behind him.

I sighed. I didn't feel like having visitors, frankly. But when I peered past the curtain separating me from the next bed, I saw a sunburned face, a long blond braid... Alicia, the whale researcher from Woods Hole!

She shuffled over to the foot of my bed. "I hope you don't mind," she said, "but I just had to come and see you.

I heard what happened to you, and…"

Mr. Peake broke in, "Alicia here contacted me, and we were both wondering — what ever happened to your friend Jesse? Did he drown? Do you know?"

Dumbstruck, I looked from one to the other. "I, uh… I don't know," I lied.

"Alicia has been doing some thinking and putting two and two together, she tells me," Mr. Peake said, giving me a very meaningful look. "She believes Jesse is the one who put her on the right track about the tsunami."

"First of all, I wanted to come and thank you," Alicia said quickly. "And Jesse too, if you know where he is. I truly think we all owe you our lives! If it hadn't been for you two…"

I stared at her.

She looked down, flustered. "But also – Well, it was uncanny, how tuned in that boy seemed to be to the whale song, so I would really like to ask him some more questions. There was something about him — I can't put my finger on it, but I just can't stop thinking about him. When I contacted Mr. Peake, he said you might have an explanation."

I glared at Mr. Peake. Why couldn't he have kept his mouth shut?

Mr. Peake shrugged. "I think it's time to come clean, Isabel," he said quietly. "Tell Alicia about Jesse. I think she deserves to know."

I shook my head, but Alicia said, "It would be such a breakthrough for us, if we could be certain somehow — if the alarm Jesse heard in the humpbacks' song was truly a warning of impending disaster. Just think what we could do with that kind of information!"

Should I tell her? Jessaloup was gone, anyway — safe in the ocean, out of harm's way. She was looking at me pleadingly. I knew she, of all people, had only the whales' best interest at heart.

"You might as well tell her," said Mr. Peake. "I have some evidence to show her, if you don't."

"What evidence?" I cried.

He looked down at the ground. "I took a picture of Jesse's hand, you know, with my cell phone, the night before the tsunami," he said sheepishly. "I thought I should document it — just in case." He fumbled in his pocket, and pulled out his phone. Cupping it in his hand so only I could see, he held it out to me.

There, indeed, was a snapshot of Jessaloup, asleep.

"What is it?" asked Alicia, excited. "Show me!"

I couldn't talk. Seeing Jessaloup lying there sleeping like an angel, his dreadlocks spread out on the pillow, his mouth slightly open, his head resting on one hand, the other hand — the flipper hand — clearly visible; it took my breath away.

Alicia snatched the cellphone out of my hand. "Ah, yes, that's him," she said. Then, peering at it more closely, she gave out a low whistle. "The hand —" she faltered. "It looks exactly like…"

"Shall I tell her, or will you?" said Mr. Peake. I stared at him, and then at Alicia, who was nodding encouragingly.

So then I just told her the whole story. Or as much as I thought Alicia had the right to know, anyway. About how Jessaloup had beached himself and turned into a human in order to warn us about the tsunami. About the quake and the tsunami being predicted in the Sirens' Song.

When I'd finished, Alicia was silent, staring at me open-mouthed.

"And when the tsunami struck, he dove into the water and turned back into a whale, and I was out on the beach because I'd run out after him, trying to get him to come back. He's the one who rescued me..." I couldn't go on, and buried my face in the pillow.

When I at last looked up, I saw my parents standing in the doorway, looking pale and wide-eyed, as if they had just seen a ghost.

forty-four

I HAD no idea how long my parents had been standing there. I started shaking. What if they'd overheard? Would they chew me out for being so irresponsible, missing the evacuation buses on purpose and running out to the beach instead of staying on higher ground? Were they furious with me, or would they just say they were "very disappointed in me," which was even worse? Would they freak out and send me to see that shrink again?

Mr. Peake greeted my parents, and walked them out of the room saying that it was getting a bit crowded in there. While the three of them chatted out in the corridor, Alicia reluctantly took her leave. "I believe you," she whispered.

"In my work with whales I've often had the feeling they were trying to communicate with us. I wouldn't put it past them, to want to warn us about the tsunami. And I did feel a strange pull to that boy — you say his real name is Jessaloup? — He felt so familiar to me. I think it's quite possible that on some unconscious level I recognized him as one of the whales I've been studying. Although I'll never be able to persuade my colleagues. They'll think I've gone off the deep end. I'd need more proof than just a fuzzy snapshot of a boy with a funny looking hand…"

I shook my head. "I can't help you," I said. "I can't give you any other proof."

"That's a shame. But — you never told me how you got involved in all this, Isabel. How did you two come to be friends?"

"It's a long story," I said quickly, because my parents and Mr. Peake were just walking back into the room. "Maybe another time."

Mr. Peake handed Alicia her shoulder bag. "Come, we ought to be going. Let's give these good folks some alone time together. Goodbye, Isabel. You are a very brave girl. I can't tell you how proud I am of you."

As they turned the corner, I saw my parents exchange a look. Mom, frowning, nodded at Dad. They both looked pretty upset. Uh-oh, I thought. Here it comes. Now I'm going to get it. How much had Mr. Peake told them?

"Darling, we need to have a serious talk."

"I don't know what you heard," I said hastily, "but I — I was just making it up. What I was telling them just now. I swear. I mean, it wasn't really like that…"

Dad coughed. Mom said, "You don't have to lie to us any more, Isabel."

I felt the tears creeping back into my eyes. I couldn't help it.

"Darling, we think we know why you're feeling like this."

I blew my nose with a loud toot to show I didn't think so.

"The doctors say that they can find nothing physically wrong with you. Except that you aren't getting better. And it's killing us."

I turned and hid my face in the pillow.

"Please. Listen to us, Isabel." Mom's voice was very serious. "There is something you should know. Dad and I — we've decided it's time to come clean. We owe you the truth."

forty-five

THE *truth!* Come *clean!* My parents had been keeping something from *me! That* made me sit up. What were they talking about? I stared at them. "Wha-what do you mean?" I stuttered, pushing the hair out of my eyes. "What truth?"

Mom gave Dad a look. "Your father has something to tell you."

I whipped my head around to look at Dad. "What, Dad? What's there to tell?"

I don't think I had ever seen my father look so upset. Taking my hand in his, he took a deep breath. "I'm sorry, babe," he said. "It's all my fault."

"What's all your fault?" I said. I had no idea what he was talking about.

Staring at the floor, he said, "I have to tell you a story."

"Go on," Mom prodded him. "Come on, James, you have to tell her."

Keeping his eyes on the floor, he said, "Well, you know, babe, that I used to go out on the ocean all the time, before you were born?"

"Yes, you used to go out in your lobster boat," I said. "When you were a lobsterman. Before you got your boring office job instead." I sighed. I never could figure out why Dad would want to work in some office, sitting at a computer all day, when he could have been at sea, cruising around on his boat in the fresh ocean air, being his own boss.

He cleared his throat. "Well, one day I set out to pull up my traps, out at Stellwagen Bank. It was foggy out, poor visibility. Normally I wouldn't have gone out in those conditions, but I had to get those traps in. When I got to the place where I'd left my buoy, I saw this whale thrashing crazily in the water, a large humpback. I quickly realized that it was caught in the line."

A humpback! I clapped my hands over my mouth.

"I didn't know what to do. I didn't want to lose my catch, but I saw that I had a big problem on my hands. The whale was spouting erratically at the surface. Blood everywhere. Then I saw that she had a calf with her, too, and it too was entangled. Maybe the mother was trying to rescue it, I don't know. All I know is that they were both in trouble. Big trouble. I could see that they would drown if I didn't do something quick."

I stared at my father in horror. "Oh, God, Dad," I gasped. "What did you *do?*"

"I got out my grappling hook, and pulled up as close as I dared. I tried to cut through the rope, but couldn't get a good handle on it. The line was wound tight around the mother's mouth — that's where all the blood was coming from — and looped around her tail. Two of my lobster cages were pinned to her back. She wouldn't stay still, and every move she made only made it worse. I finally did manage to cut through the line, releasing my traps, but it was no use, she was still caught, twisted in that rope like a lassoed steer."

He stopped, and looked up at my mother.

"Go on," she said quietly. "Tell her the whole story."

I patted Dad's hand, my head in a whirl. "Yes, go on," I said. "You can tell me."

He shook his head. "I wasn't able to save her. It was too late. She was already too weak by the time I got there. She'd lost so much blood. Just as I was radioing for help, I — I saw her blow for the last time, and then she sank..."

He was silent. Mom and I were silent too. I gulped, thinking, *Who was it? Was she a member of my pod? What calf? How come Dad never talked about this before?*

"What about the calf?" I said. "Did the calf drown too?"

Dad shook his head. "I — I'm not sure. But that's the thing, see. When I finally hauled in what was left of my traps…" He stopped, unable to go on.

"What?" I said anxiously. "What, Dad?"

"It sounds crazy, I know. But there was a baby in one."

"A *baby!*"

"Dripping wet, but alive."

"But how…"

"A pretty human baby, looking at me with her big brown eyes." He gazed at me helplessly. "She stretched out her little arms, as if to say, *Pick me up, Daddy.* So I did."

I whirled around to stare at Mom. She had tears in her eyes.

"What's he saying!" I cried. "Who — was that, was that…"

Mom nodded. "It was. That was you. Our little miracle."

forty-six

I was stunned. I couldn't speak. I couldn't breathe. I couldn't think.

"You mean you're — you're not my real parents?" I finally managed.

Dad cleared his throat. "Not your biological parents, no. We should have told you, babe, but we didn't know how..."

"We were just so grateful to have you," Mom whispered. "We had been trying for a girl, but it just wasn't happening. I mean, we did love our two boys, of course, but we had so wanted a little girl as well..."

"You were the joy of our lives," Dad interrupted her. "We didn't ask any questions, we just accepted it. A gift from God. The answer to our prayers. You were so adorable."

I collapsed backwards on the bed, dizzy with all this new, shocking information.

"We tried to forget about where you'd come from. You grew into a normal little girl. It wasn't until you disappeared, on that fifth-grade whale watch, that we began to wonder if we had done the right thing, keeping you…"

"Deepanorah," I whispered.

"What did you say?"

"I think I know who my real mother was," I said. I didn't know if I was angry — *furious!* — or happy — deliriously happy. "You should have told me. It would have explained everything. I've been so confused!"

"We didn't want to lose you again, my love. Please understand! That year, when you went missing, we kept hoping and praying that you would come back to us."

"And then, when our prayers were answered, babe, and you were home safe and sound again, we thought that it was meant to be, and so we did everything we could to have everything go back to normal."

"*Normal? What's* normal?" I cried, sitting up again. "What's normal to you isn't at all normal to me! I've been so miserable these past three years! And now I know why. I don't really belong here! I'm sorry, Mom, Dad, and I know you meant well, but it wasn't *right* of you not to tell me!"

"We know that now, darling. We're so sorry. We know now that we were wrong." Mom was crying, tears rolling down her face. Dad went over to her and started rubbing her shoulder awkwardly. He cleared his throat, and said huskily, "But it seems that you haven't been exactly straight with us, either, Isabel."

I shook my head. "I guess it's time for me to stop lying too."

"No more secrets?" said Mom.

"No more secrets," I said.

forty-seven

My parents arranged to have me discharged from the hospital a few days later, even though I was still weak and wobbly and couldn't really walk on my own. Whenever I tried to stand up, my legs would buckle under me; every step felt as if I were walking on sharp knives.

I was struggling with wild mood swings, too — one moment I'd be euphoric at the thought that I had been born in the sea, a true Siren child (now I finally understood why I had been so drawn to the whales my whole life!), and the next I'd be down in the dumps again. For here I was, a weak, human girl, separated from my ocean home forever.

I finally told Mom and Dad the whole story — all my adventures in the ocean, both the first time, when I had fallen overboard and turned into a whale, and the second time, after the tsunami, when I hadn't. I tried not to leave anything out. They listened silently for the most part, except for the occasional question. That was the weirdest thing for me — they didn't seem to be at all surprised. And to think that all this time I had kept it a secret, convinced that they would think I was completely out of my mind!

They insisted that I tell Jacob and Alex as well. "We're a family," said my father, "and I think we have to talk this over as a family."

It was a relief to be able to get it all off my chest, though my brothers wouldn't believe it at first. "You're kidding, right, Dad?" they said. "Mom, is she serious? Is she telling the truth?"

When they finally got used to the idea that their sister had been a whale, they started off giving me a hard time about it. Of course. "I *knew* your story sucked," said Alex. "About how you managed to swim to a desert island after you fell overboard, and stayed alive living off berries and stuff. And then how you made yourself a raft. That made no sense. I mean, even with survival-skills training, a girl like you couldn't possibly…"

"Oh yeah?" I cried. Alex always knew how to get my goat. "You have no idea what a girl like me is capable of!"

"Hey, come on, chill," said Jacob. "Anyway, I think it's really cool the way you stopped that whaling ship by ramming a mast into the propeller. Quick thinking, Izza.

I'm proud of you."

"Yeah," said Alex, slapping me on the back. "I always knew you had it in you."

"Far out," said Jacob, whistling under his breath, "my little sister, a whale…! I can't believe it!'"

Alex and Dad carried me upstairs to Sea World, my green turret-room, and installed me in a lounge chair in front of the window, with a pair of binoculars, so I could look out at the sea. Jacob got Mr. Peake to email the photo of Jessaloup asleep, and printed it out for me.

Whenever I looked at that picture (which was very often), the tears would return.

Those days were long and dreary. I couldn't do much — my eyes were too weak to read or to write anything. Nothing interested me except for the CD of whale songs that Alicia dropped off for me one day; I listened to it for hours as I watched the neighbors on our street clean up their yards and sweep away the debris the tsunami had left behind. The hardware store across the street had reopened and was doing a booming business; I saw customers loading their trucks with sheetrock, lumber, dehumidifiers, pumps and gallons of paint. New trees and bushes were being planted to replace the ones that had been destroyed. Slowly but surely, the neighborhood was starting to come to life again.

But not me. My skin color didn't improve: it looked very grey, with peeling and flaking patches all over, and I was still losing weight. I just didn't feel like eating. The only thing I had any appetite for was fried clams and clam chowder, neither of which I'd been at all fond of before, but which my mother was now glad to bring up to my room on a tray. "Eat," she urged me. "Eat, Isabel, or you'll waste away to nothing!"

Meanwhile my brothers and father were busy with some secret project they wouldn't tell me about, acting all sneaky and mysterious about it. I knew that dropping hints about it was the only way they could think of to make me snap out of my lethargy: I used to love surprises.

"Wait until it's finished, Fish-Face," they promised. "Wait until you see. You won't believe your eyes."

"Oh yeah?" I said listlessly. "Great." I couldn't even bring up the indignation to bristle at this new nickname they had come up with for me, since they were doing their very best to cheer me up.

Alex announced that he had decided on a major in college — biology, with a minor in environmental studies. He was going to be a marine biologist, "Because I can't think of anything that interests me more. I've been talking to your friend Alicia. I think what she's doing is really cool. You don't mind, do you?" he asked solicitously, "because I know that's what you always said you wanted to be when you grew up too."

I shook my head, and grimaced. "The more marine biologists, the merrier," I assured him. Turning to Jacob, I said, "How about it, Jake?

"Why not?" Jacob said. "We'll make it the family business!"

forty-eight

FINALLY the big day came — they were going to show me my surprise. Dad carried me downstairs, where I was expecting to find something tied with a big bow — a dollhouse they'd built, maybe, or a fish tank, or a puppy, or even a wheelchair, since my legs were still not working properly. Instead they loaded me into Mom's car and tied a bandana around my eyes so that I couldn't see where we were going.

"Here we are. You can take off your blindfold," Alex instructed me.

I looked around. We were at the old wharf. Or rather, where it used to be. The wharf was gone except for a few pylons strewn around higgledy-piggledy; a brand new concrete pier, half-finished, was sticking out into the ocean. Seeing the wrecked fisherman's shack, the roof and two walls gone, made me start crying again.

"Chill, Isabel," urged Jacob, "look over there!"

It was Dad's old boat. But instead of sitting propped up on blocks behind the shack, it was tied up to a dock, bobbing up and down in the water. And instead of rotten boards and peeling paint, it looked brand new, sparkling in the sun. Its hull was dark blue, the wheelhouse had been painted white with aqua trim, and the railing had been polished to a fine gleam.

"Wow," I said through my tears. "You've fixed up the *Clorinda*. It's beautiful, Dad. Really beautiful."

"After the tsunami, guess where she ended up!" said Jacob excitedly.

I shrugged. "I don't know."

"Right at the foot of the Pilgrim Tower!" said Jacob. "The wave picked her up and left her up there on the hill, lying on her side. But she wasn't smashed to pieces like a lot of the other boats. She was still whole!"

"Everyone said it was miraculous. It made us feel we *had* to make her seaworthy again," said Alex.

"We've been waiting for you to take her on her maiden voyage," said Dad. "Your brothers persuaded me to do this. For you."

"We had to rebuild the engine," boasted Alex. "And clean out the mess left by the gulls and mice."

"It was gross," said Jacob.

I didn't know what to say. "Thanks, Dad, thanks, Alex, thank you, Jacob," I managed. "It's fantastic. You're the best."

"Come on," said Dad. "Boys, let's carry her on board."

forty-nine

WHEN I was safely installed on a bench in the stern, they cast off. For the first time in months, I actually felt a thrill of excitement.

The engine, after roaring noisily out of the harbor, settled down into a hypnotic, throaty hum, like one of Gram's cats purring. It was a glorious day. I took in grateful gulps of the salt air, and stared down at the shimmering sea that folded back so obediently on either side of the prow. It reminded me of…

Mom came and sat next to me. "Isn't this nice?" she said. I nodded, but didn't look up. I kept my eyes on the water.

"Is that where you want to be?" she whispered sadly, following my gaze.

I shook my head. The truth was that I longed to be there, that I'd much rather be down there in the water than up here, high and dry with my human family, who were trying so hard to please me. But I couldn't tell her that. The thought of how she'd feel if she knew made my heart ache even more than it already did.

Mom waved at Dad, who was standing at the wheel. He said, "Here, Alex, you take over for a bit." He came and sat beside us, and peered out at the sea.

"Where are we going, Dad?" I asked. At the same time, Mom said, with concern in her voice, "How are you doing, James?"

"I'm OK," he told her grimly.

I felt a pang of alarm. Was there something they weren't telling me?

Turning to me, Dad said, "We're heading for Stellwagen Bank. The last place this old boat and I ever visited. The place where I... you know... found you, babe."

"Oh," I said. "OK. So you really never took the boat out to sea again? After that?"

"After finding you? That's right. I never went out again."

I was quiet for a moment, but then I couldn't help asking, "Why not?"

"I haven't told you everything," he replied, raising his voice to be heard over the noise of the wind, which was picking up. "I suppose I should tell you now."

I nodded, wide-eyed. My brothers too were craning their necks to hear.

Dad cleared his throat. With another look at Mom, he said, "Well, after recovering from the shock of having a dying whale on my hands..." — he hesitated, then corrected himself — "...the shock of having a dead whale on my *conscience*, because really it was all my fault that she died, and then the even bigger shock of finding a baby in my trap, I started for shore as fast as I could. I wrapped you in my yellow slicker; I was afraid you'd catch cold. But then..." He stopped, and swallowed.

"Then what, Dad?" Jacob urged him.

"I realized I was being followed."

"You were being followed?" Jacob exclaimed. "By what, Dad? Who?"

Dad was peering down at the water, as if he could still see it. "Whales. Dozens of them. I've never seen anything like it. Following the boat, like a procession. It was as if they were escorting me on my way. Only I wasn't sure if that was what they were doing. I wasn't sure they were friendly. I thought, 'Maybe they're going to attack me.' You know, because I had killed one of them, with my gear. So — I panicked. I gunned the engine, and didn't look back until I was in the harbor."

"Wow, Dad," said Alex, shaking his head. "But did they? Did they attack? What did you do?"

"No. They left me alone, thank goodness. But, you know, I felt so bad about the whole thing that I sold my traps to Tim Crosby the next day. And I never went out in my boat again." After another long pause, he admitted, "I guess I was scared."

He got up, turning his back on us. "I don't want you kids to think your Dad is a coward…"

"No of course we don't think that!" we all protested.

"I just didn't know what would happen," he went on, "if I went back out to sea. If they would find me and confront me or anything. Or demand their baby back. And now we'll see, won't we." He stopped; but no one could think of anything to say, so he went on, "My thinking is, if we head out to the spot where I found Isabel, maybe the whales will come. And then maybe Isabel will know what to do."

I stared at him open-mouthed.

"I mean, what to say to them — how to let them know how sorry I am for what happened," he said. Then he ducked back under the roof of the wheelhouse and took over the tiller from Alex.

My heart melted. He looked so stern, so determined, standing there.

And, suddenly, I felt stronger. Much stronger. Dad needed me. He needed me to tell him the whales would forgive him. But… how could I promise him that, when I had no way of knowing how the whales really felt about it?

I didn't know what to tell him. I turned to him. "*I* forgive you, anyway, Dad," I said carefully. "Because you *thought* you were doing the right thing."

Mom squeezed my hand gratefully.

We all fell silent, busy with our own thoughts, as the *Clorinda* chugged on toward her destination: Stellwagen Bank.

fifty

"OK, here we are," announced my father. He cut the engine, which wound down with a few final clicks, then fell silent, so that you could hear the waves slapping against the hull. Dad was showing Alex the location on the chart in the wheelhouse. "See? That's Stellwagen there. Close enough, anyway, I think."

My heart was banging so loudly against my eardrums that I almost couldn't hear. Trembling with excitement, I grabbed hold of the metal rail and hauled myself up, so that I was kneeling on the bench on my shaky knees, leaning out.

"Careful!" warned my mother. "Isabel, you're too weak — you might fall!" She put her arm around my waist, holding me tight. I didn't shrug her off, grateful for the support.

There was nothing out there but the silver water, rising and falling, like row upon row of sleeping bodies breathing in, breathing out.

Minutes went by. I squinted at the horizon. I peered into the water right under my nose, but I couldn't see a thing, because the sky's reflection made it hard to see anything below the indifferent, dancing surface.

What was I supposed to *do*?

I cleared my throat. I took a breath. "*Sirens! Whales!*" I called out faintly, "I'm here! It's me, Isabel, the Mermaid!"

Still nothing but open water, and a few curious sea gulls circling overhead.

"Jessaloup!" I cried, louder now. "Onijonah! Can you hear me?"

"Don't excite yourself too much, babe," said Dad. "If they come, they come. We'll wait. We can stay here all day if we have to. If that's what you think we should do."

"I don't know… I don't know!" I was near tears again, crushed with disappointment at not seeing any of my whales. "I mean — I don't know if they're even in the area. They could be miles away, miles and miles away, up north, where the best feeding grounds are." What made me think that Jessaloup would just be hanging around our coast waiting for me to show up in a boat? Or the other members of our pod, for that matter? What made me think I was so special, anyway?

Gliding along parallel to the horizon, the flimsy, lazy clouds stretched and lengthened. I felt a pang of envy. Those clouds didn't have any doubts about where they were going, or what they were supposed to do. Unlike me.

Just as I was turning around to rest my numb knees, I heard a shout from Jacob, who was standing on the bow.

"What?" I yelled back.

"Over there! Look!"

And sure enough, I heard the familiar *whoosh*, and smelled the fishy smell of a whale exhaling. I would know that sound, that smell, anywhere.

"Jessaloup!" I cried, sticking my head out as far as I dared through the space between the gunwale and the safety railing. "You *did* come! You heard me!" But Jessaloup, if that was him, was no longer there — he had dived smoothly under the boat. He would be resurfacing at any moment on the other side. I pulled my head back in and stumbled over to the starboard side, ignoring the stabbing pains in my feet and calves. "Isabel!" my mother cried. "Don't! Careful!"

"Look!" my brothers were shouting. "There! And there! And over there!"

Pull yourself together, I told myself. *Don't embarrass yourself. Show some dignity.* Dragging myself to a standing position, holding on to the railing, I looked out at what just a moment ago had been an empty sea.

And sure enough: it was a rolling, snorting, fizzing frenzy out there. Slithery grey and black backs, and fins of every shape and size, as far as the eye could see. In less than a minute I was drenched. I looked back at my family, the four of them huddled together now under the wheelhouse canopy. "Don't worry," I yelled at them, grinning from ear to ear. "They don't mean any harm. It's a gathering. This is what they do."

"But…" stammered Jacob, "there's so many of them!"

"I know," I said. "But it's good. It means they are expecting something to happen."

"What…?" my mother started asking anxiously, but I shushed her.

"They're friendly," I said. "Don't worry." I felt completely in control now. And my legs seemed to be getting their strength back.

I climbed onto the gunwale. "Who's there?" I called out. "Onijonah, is that you?"

I heard a loud blow, like a sneeze, and I saw my guardian's dear mottled back just below me. "Can you understand what I'm saying?"

"I understand, Merchild," I heard. "And I see that you have not forgotten our whale-tongue."

"Oh, Onijonah," I cried. "I'm so happy to see you! Who else is here — Is that… can that be Mistenbel?" A young humpback a few rows back was spy-hopping with her head sticking straight up in the air, which is like treading water for us. "Hey, Mistenbel! You're such a big whale now! Do you remember me? You were just a baby when I left!" I shouted, wiping the spray from my eyes. "Greetings, everyone! Oh, you're all here! You've all come! I've missed you so very much!"

"What are you saying?" hissed Alex. "Why are you making those funny noises? Are you talking to them? Can they hear you?"

"Of course they can hear me," I answered over my shoulder. "Shut up a minute, will you? Let me talk to them."

"Merchild," rumbled Onijonah. "We are all here. We knew you would come here today. It was in the Song."

I took a deep, rattling breath. I didn't know where to begin. I tried not to lose sight of Jessaloup, who was keeping his distance from the boat, swimming up and down excitedly and causing a commotion, because there really wasn't much room to maneuver out there without bumping into other whales.

Suddenly I knew what to say. "Elders, whales, I humbly thank you for coming. I suppose I ought to introduce my family first," — I gestured at the four bewildered humans behind me — "My mother and father, Ellen and James, and my brothers, Jacob and Alex."

Dozens of whale voices responded politely in chorus.

"We have come," I went on, "because my father has something to say to you."

I waved Dad over, and he stepped over some life vests to stand at my side. "You tell them what you have to say to them," I said, "and I'll translate for you. OK?"

He nodded, and coughed into his fist. "Ladies and gentlemen," he started, then whispered to me, "is that the right form of address? I don't know what else to call them."

"Don't worry," I said. "Go on, I'll put it into their language."

"Ladies and gentlemen," he said. "I owe you a great apology —"

"She-whales and he-whales," I translated, *"my father is very, very sorry."*

"— as well as my most profound condolences," he went on.

"And, uh, his heart is heavy for you," I told them.

"Because, fifteen years ago, a whale got tangled up in my gear," Dad said. "By accident."

"Fifteen summers ago, one of your sisters was accidentally caught in his rope," I explained.

"And I was unable to cut her loose," he went on. "Although I did my best."

"And he couldn't save her," I said. *"But he did try."*

The whales spouted softly, almost in unison. "Tell James," said Onijonah, "that we know that he speaks the truth. He tried to save her."

I told Dad what she said. He was quiet a while, letting it sink in. Then, bowing his head, he went on, "In that case I hope that they'll forgive me —"

"We have long forgiven him," came the reply.

"I'll do anything, anything at all to make it up to you," he said humbly.

"There is no need. For he has already repaid us. He has done us the greatest favor in all the world."

"What's she saying?" asked Dad, because I was suddenly staring at Onijonah, thunderstruck.

"You're forgiven," I said hastily. "Uh — Just a minute, Dad. I have to ask her something first."

I reached my hand out over the side of the boat to touch the side of Onijonah's majestic head. "Onijonah," I whispered. "What's this greatest favor? What favor are you talking about?"

She did not reply at once.

"Was it — was it Deepanorah who died?" I asked, trembling.

There was a long silence. Finally someone else spoke up — it was Momboduno, grunting in his gravelly voice, "Deepanorah was Onijonah's sister. That is why it is hard for her to speak of this."

"Let me tell her, Momboduno," said Onijonah. "Yes, Merchild. It was she."

"And was — was Deepanorah my mother?"

I heard a rattling sob — the sound a Siren makes when overcome with emotion. "Ah, Merchild, so you know! Yes, she was your mother."

"But how — why…"

"What are they saying?" urged Mom. "What are you talking about?" *Not now,* I told her with a wave of my arm. *Wait.*

"She knew that she was lost. But she was determined to save her child. So she took a chance, and offered her calf — you, Merchild — to James, your human father."

"But… But what was the favor? I don't understand —"

"That was the favor, Isabel. The moment he saw you, he took you in his arms. We hoped — we *knew* — that he would take good care of you. If you had remained in the sea without your mother, without any mother's milk, you would have died for lack of nourishment. We followed James back to shore, to manifest our gratitude. We hoped that he would return often, to show us how you were growing. But he never came back."

"I know," I said. "He was afraid. He didn't understand."

"We never gave up hope, however, that we would see you again. We inspected every ship that set out from this shore, to no avail. Until…"

"Until the day I did come, on board that whale watching boat," I said. "When I was eleven."

"That is correct, Merchild. And you know the rest."

I needed a few moments to let it all sink in. But I wasn't done yet. There were still pieces of the puzzle missing. More indignant questions bubbling up inside me.

"But why — if I really belong in the ocean, why am I still a *girl*?" I cried, gripping the handrail and shaking it.

"When you first came back to us, Merchild, you were torn. You missed your human family. It would not have been fair to make that decision for you, before you possessed the wisdom to make it for yourself."

"I…" I began, but Onijonah went on, "And then, of course, when you proved yourself so brave, saving Mistenbel and me from the harpooners, and you were injured, we could not allow you to remain a whale. You would have died of your wounds. So we made you beach yourself and return to human form."

"OK, I get that," I said. "But what about now? I think

I'm wise enough now to make my own decisions."

"Perhaps you are," she allowed.

"So — but, see, when the tsunami…" I had to swallow hard before I could make myself go on, "I mean, in the tsunami, Jessaloup turned back into a whale. But I DIDN'T!" The unfairness of it all made me want to scream, but it came out sounding more like a wail. "*Why* couldn't I have stayed in the ocean *this* time? What would have been so wrong with *that?*"

I heard some sputtering and pinging. Onijonah was conferring with the elders, and they didn't want me to hear.

I turned to my family, and whispered, "It's all being explained. It's all right, though. I'll tell you in a minute, OK?"

"Which one is Jessaloup?" asked Jacob. I pointed him out to my brothers. Jessaloup was still zigzagging in and out of the throng of whalebacks, flapping his flukes, leaping in the air, slapping his fins on the surface, and generally making a nuisance of himself. "The crazy one? I thought it might be!" Jacob said. "Awesome!"

Finally Onijonah spoke up again. "Remember that I said that your father James had done us a favor in taking you and raising you as his own?"

"Yes," I said.

"It would not have been right if you had disappeared again just like that, without any explanation. It was hard enough for your human family the first time. It would have been a terrible blow, to lose you a second time. They would not have known that you were not dead. Their grief would have been unending. They would have been heartbroken."

"You're right," I said guiltily. "I guess I never thought of it like that."

And then Onijonah said something that changed everything.

She said, "So you see. We cannot let you return to us, Merchild, until *they* are ready to let you go."

fifty-one

THE sun was low in the sky; the wind was getting a little cooler. Mom shivered and pulled her windbreaker on. The sky was streaked with spectacular pinks and purples. Shafts of yellow light poured down from gaps in the golden-edged clouds, like in a biblical painting. We were sitting in a little circle in the stern, our arms around each other, our heads almost touching. Dad was stroking my hair. I had just finished telling them what Onijonah had said to me, and I saw that everyone's eyes were damp.

"Well now," said Dad in a hoarse voice. "I think we know what we have to do."

Mom wiped away a tear. "I know. The time has come. We have to let you go, if that is what you want."

There was a gasp.

"Wait — you can't be serious!" cried Jacob. "Let her go? You mean… But she's our sister, she belongs with us!"

Mom shushed him, saying, "It comes as a shock to you now, darling, because we never told you about the way Isabel came into our lives. But in a way, your father and I had been expecting something like this. We always knew Isabel didn't belong to us a hundred percent."

"We were always afraid that the sea would reclaim her some day," said Dad quietly. "And now that day is here. And we have to be prepared to let her go."

"No!" said Jacob. "That's not fair!"

"It's Isabel's life," said Mom, "and it is her decision to make, darling. Let's give her that choice."

"But…" protested Alex, "can't she… Couldn't she just visit the whales once in a while, by boat, like today? Are you saying you're all *right* with her turning back into a *whale?*"

"It doesn't matter what *we're* all right with. The point is, what's right for her, Alex. You must know that, in your heart."

"Why can't it wait? Why now?" Jacob said.

"Look at her, Jacob. See how grey she is, how weak. Can't you see? She's wasting away. She's so unhappy. The doctors said she might never have the use of her legs again. They said she might die."

I listened to them in a daze. What did I want? Hearing them argue over me, my heart was just bursting with love for all four of them.

Suddenly the boat shook. I looked over the side, and saw that someone had rammed us — deliberately. I heard Onijonah scolding, "*Jessaloup!* Can't you be just a little more patient? Leave her alone!"

"Hey, Jessaloup," I called out shyly. "Is that you?"

"Yeah, it's me. What's taking so long? What are they arguing about?"

"They're not arguing. They're talking about letting me go."

I said it — and what I had just said hung in the air.

My heart made a big leap as the reality of it suddenly sank in. "Jessaloup, Onijonah," I cried, "I think they're ready to let me go! What should I *do?*"

"Jump!" came the prompt reply. From Jessaloup, of course.

I looked back at my family sitting there staring at me. "Are you really sure… I can go?" I faltered.

Mom and Dad nodded bravely. Alex gave me the thumbs-up and from Jacob came a sullen "I s'ppose".

I kneeled on the gunwale, and started pulling myself up. The rippling water beckoned. I felt a hundred whale eyes on me.

"Wait!" I said, turning back to my family. "I almost forgot. I need a hug."

"Thought you'd never ask," smiled my dad through his tears.

We fumbled our way into a group hug. They squeezed me so hard that I could barely breathe.

"If this works," I whispered, "if I do turn back into a whale, promise me that you'll come see me some time."

"How will we find you?" Jacob choked.

I looked around. The ocean was all grand, grey infinity. Nothing but sea, sky, the setting sun…

The sun!

"*I* know," I said. "The solstice. A year from now. The whales have a different calendar, but the longest day is the same for us as for you. So on the day of the solstice, every year from now on, I'll come looking for the *Clorinda*. I promise. Look out for a grey humpback with curvy flukes, shaped like a heart. That'll be me."

"But — how will we know it's really *you*?" said Mom.

"You'll know," I said. "You'll just know."

And then I climbed onto the bow, stepped over the railing, took a deep breath, and jumped.

THEY *are nearly Home.*

The migration south has taken the better part of two months, but from the taste of the water they can tell that they are near. The females and yearlings have stayed in a close-knit group; the males stray farther afield, although always within easy hearing range.

Together they have plowed through vicious storms and skimmed over calm seas. They have found their way by following the arc of the sun in the sky and by listening to the silent song inside their heads. They have grazed the tops of ocean peaks taller than the tallest mountain, and crossed canyons so deep that no whale has ever plumbed their depths. They have glimpsed sea monsters unknown to man and seen a thousand miracles.

The swaying kelp forests have given way to undulating meadows of sea grass, where the darting fishes play hide and seek and tiny seahorses twirl across the floor. They are in warmer waters now; the coral reefs beckon. Home! The mother whales leave the pack to scout out a quiet patch of ocean where they will give birth when the time comes.

There is a fizz of excitement in the water. The young whales can't help themselves, they leap and twist and roll around in the sun-heated surf. Some of their games end in violent scuffles, when several males pursue the same female and must fight for her attentions. But there is one young whale who does not need to prove himself in a fight. The other males have agreed to leave him alone, for he has long since earned his prize.

"Wha... what's that?" the yearlings ask their mothers. *"Did you hear that?"*

"Hush, children, run along and play. That song isn't meant for little ears."

And somewhere deep beneath the sea, the mermaid lets herself drift on the rippling currents, now warm, now cool, now strong, now faint. Her eyes are closed, and she listens, spellbound, with every fiber of her body. Here, finally, is the sound she has been waiting for so long:

The Siren serenade, the sweetest melody, the music of her dreams...

Jessaloup's Song.

Come, dear children, let us away;
Down and away below!
Now my brothers call from the bay,
Now the great winds shoreward blow,
Now the salt tides seaward flow;
Now the wild white horses play,
Champ and chafe and toss in the spray.
Children dear, let us away!
Children dear, was it yesterday
We heard the sweet bells over the bay?
In the caverns where we lay,
Through the surf and through the swell,
The far-off sound of a silver bell?

Sand-strewn caverns, cool and deep,
Where the winds are all asleep;
Where the spent lights quiver and gleam,
Where the salt weed sways in the stream,
Where the sea-beasts, ranged all round,
Feed in the ooze of their pasture-ground;
Where the sea-snakes coil and twine,
Dry their mail and bask in the brine;
Where great whales come sailing by,
Sail and sail, with unshut eye,
Round the world for ever and aye?
When did music come this way?
Children dear, was it yesterday?

— from *The Forsaken Merman* by
Matthew Arnold (1822–1888)

HESTER VELMANS grew up in the Netherlands, along the dunes at the edge of the North Sea. An award-winning translator, today she lives inland, on a farm in Massachusetts, where she often dreams of the sea.

The first book in the series, *Isabel of the Whales*, an "eco-romance," was a surprise national best-seller.